AFTER THE FLOOD

Praise for *Fish* by L.S. Matthews:

'An allegory grounded in remarkably tactile storytelling . . . Matthews allows just enough detail – and heart – to make miracles feel possible.' *Publishers Weekly*

'The fable-like quality of the telling has a subdued power.' Linda Newbery, *TES*

'Stunning debut novel' *The Glasgow Herald*

Books by L.S. Matthews:

Fish
WINNER OF THE FIDLER AWARD
HIGHLY COMMENDED FOR THE
BRANFORD BOASE AWARD

The Outcasts
SHORTLISTED FOR THE NASEN AWARD

A Dog for Life

Lexi

AFTER THE FLOOD

L. S. Matthews

Hodder
Children's
Books

A division of Hachette Children's Books

To all the horses who have taught me so much,
especially Bree, who explained to me about the
blinkers, and to Pinky, the Ardennes cross,
who introduced me to this wonderful breed.

Text copyright © 2008 L.S. Matthews

First published in Great Britain in 2008
by Hodder Children's Books

The rights of L.S. Matthews to be identified as the Author of
the Work has been asserted by her in accordance with the
Copyright, Designs and Patents Act 1988.

1

A Catalogue record for this book is available
from the British Library

ISBN-13: 978 0 340 93181 3

Typeset in New Baskerville and Tekton by Avon DataSet Ltd,
Bidford on Avon, Warwickshire

Printed and bound in Great Britain by
CPI Bookmarque, Croydon, CR0 4TD

The paper and board used in this paperback by
Hodder Children's Books are natural recyclable products made
from wood grown in sustainable forests. The manufacturing
processes conform to the environmental regulations
of the country of origin.

Hodder Children's Books
A division of Hachette Children's Books
338 Euston Road, London NW1 3BH
An Hachette Livre UK Company

1

It's the Sea

When did I first realise that something was wrong?

I was watching my dad putting on his coat. It was late evening and there had been yet another flood warning. These were very boring. Like a lot of other people in the village of Ingwick, we had actually packed up all our stuff three times and left our house. We had gathered at the school or at the village's only hotel and, three times, nothing had happened.

Dad was working on flood defences, and had said every time that they would hold, and he should know. And he was right, of course, they had held.

All these warnings caused the problem that night. Outside, in the dark, winter's night, a bitterly cold January wind was gripping our world with its teeth. It shook and worried at the trees till they groaned along with its howling. No one would want to go out into that. I'd never heard anything like it. Maybe that was it, thinking back – the first sign I'd had that something was wrong, different, from all the times we'd been warned before. Mum had phoned around and found out that some people weren't keen to evacuate this time. She'd persuaded most, but not the old couple, Mr and Mrs Downes, who lived a few doors away, despite begging and pleading.

'This is crazy,' Dad was saying to Mum. 'We should have gone by now. We can't stay around wasting time. Everyone else will have to make their own decisions. I'll go and help the Downes, you get packed up here. I'll be right back.'

'But what if they won't change their minds?' asked Mum.

My dad sighed.

'Val, they're very old, very tiny, and very frail. If need be, I will pick them up and carry them out by force, one under each arm.'

Mum laughed and smacked at him as he headed to the front door. 'They'd never speak to you again if you did that! Can you imagine?'

He pecked her on the cheek as he went through the door, the wind screeching into the hall.

'Somehow I'd live with that,' he said, disappearing into the night. The Downes were very sweet but could keep you talking for hours if they caught you as you passed their garden. That's how Mum and Dad had got to know them.

Me and Mum and Dad had lived in Ingwick for about a year. Before that, we'd lived in other towns and villages on the east coast, always near the sea. My dad, you see, was a special engineer, working on sea and flood defences, so we went where his job took him. Mum was OK about moving – she taught violin at schools and gave private lessons too, so she could carry on with that pretty much wherever we went. I had got used to leaving friends, which was sad, but you could look forward to making new ones. I didn't like school much, so never minded leaving.

Dad and Mum had explained to me that Ingwick had been flooded years ago in some big storm, along with loads of other places, and because they weren't good at warning people back then, lots of people had died. Despite the great work on the sea defences, this was why the people in charge of such things were now a little hasty with warnings.

I was slightly on the side of the Downes, it has to be said. I didn't want to pack things up and then go out into that freezing night to the hotel or wherever; but no one was asking me what I thought. I don't know why, but tonight I went to the lounge window to watch Dad go down the path.

I could just about see him in the light from the porch steps, buffeted by the wind, his gloved hand gripping the scarf at his throat to keep it there. His feet splashed in a puddle when he got to the front gate, and then he did something strange.

He took off one of his gloves, bent down, dipped his finger in the puddle and put it to his mouth.

Then he straightened up and looked back towards the house, and his eyes found me, watching from the window. Then he seemed to look beyond me, and I was aware of Mum at my shoulder. I turned to her.

But she had gone, and I heard her open the

front door. The shrieking of the wind instantly filled the house.

I looked back out at Dad.

He was cupping his mouth, calling against the wind to Mum at the front door.

Then he turned and was through the gate, away and lost into the dark night.

I heard Mum close the door and instantly the roar of the storm was quieter.

'What was he doing?' I called, running to her. 'What did he say?'

'It's the sea.' Her voice faltered. 'He said it's come.'

2

The Roar

I hardly had time to think what this meant, or what it would mean. Mum was telling me to grab things and take them upstairs to put on the beds. She filled a flask of water and pushed it into my hands. This seemed the strangest thing at the time, but I did not question anything. I just did as I was told.

As we came back downstairs from putting a load of coats and boxes of photos on my bed, we both saw the trickle of water feeling its way, like a tentacle, under the front door. We paused for a moment, then Mum bustled me into the kitchen, where she made me pull on my wellingtons while she grabbed things in a calm but hurried way and loaded me with them as if I were a pack mule.

'That's enough now,' said Mum, pushing the mobile phone into my hand, along with two woolly hats, her violin in its case, and a little painting her mother had given her.

At that moment, the mobile trilled and lit up in my hand.

We froze – we weren't used to using it very often as it was expensive. Despite the stuff in my arms, I managed to press the button and put it to my ear.

'It's First Alert here,' shouted a man's voice. 'Is that James Crosby?'

'No, it's his son,' I answered, and was about to ask if whoever it was wanted to speak to Mum, but the voice just carried on as if I hadn't spoken.

'Catastrophic failure of the sea wall at Chich. That village is drowned. Now it's heading your way across the marshes.'

'Thank you, I'll tell him, but I think he knows . . .' The line was dead.

I looked at Mum.

'What?' she asked fearfully.

'It was the warning team for Dad. Chich has gone.' I couldn't use the word 'drowned', though I knew people just used it to mean 'flooded'. Thank goodness it wasn't us, I thought. Chich was over three miles away. I'd walked three miles so I knew it was a long way.

'Then your dad was right. *Our* sea defences *have* held. But it's broken through there and is coming across the land for us anyway,' said Mum. I heard a note of defeat in her voice.

She gave herself a little shake.

'Put these on our bed, then find all the warm clothes you can and put them on. All of them. Jumpers, socks, your waterproof coat, the lot.' As she spoke, she was dragging on her coat and struggling with her boots. I couldn't help but notice she seemed to be hurrying. 'Wait for me up there. Don't come back downstairs.'

'But where are you going?' I asked as she followed me to the hall, giving me a gentle shove towards the stairs. Already there were a couple of centimetres of water spreading slowly along the floor.

'I'm just going to tie the boat up so it doesn't float off,' she said.

'Oh,' I said. 'Good idea.'

I headed up the stairs, trying not to drop things,

pleased and a little surprised Mum had thought to save the boat. It was only a small wooden one for rowing, with a mast for sailing in the right weather, but we'd had some fun in it. I had a fleeting worry about my skateboard, out in the garden. Oh well, it would probably dry out OK.

'Jack?' she called after me, when I was half way up the stairs.

'Yes?'

'When you get up there, open our bedroom window, would you?'

'OK,' I answered cheerfully.

I dumped all the stuff Mum had piled into my arms on their bed, went into my room and got all my warmest gear and brought it back there, and then remembered what she'd said about the window.

Open the window? Still, I pushed back the curtains, just as a squall of sleet slammed into the pane of glass with such a whack I thought it would shatter. Outside, it was now pitch black, and I couldn't see a thing. I grabbed hold of the handle of the window, but trying to open it was a battle. An invisible and powerful shoulder seemed to do its best to shut it in my face, or else fling it back and off its hinges.

Finally I had it hooked open, and now the screaming and roaring of the wind was incredibly loud, filling the room. As I dragged on layer after layer of warm clothes, I could hear another note, low and droning like an old-fashioned freight train or a plane, and knew, somehow, that it wasn't the wind.

Dressed so I could hardly bend my elbows or knees, I waddled to the window again – where was Mum?

I leaned out as far as I dared; instantly the wind screeched around me, gripped my head, sucked the breath from my body. I couldn't tell if it was me swaying, or the house. I felt as if I were on a ship. Sleet slapped me like the spray of breaking waves. I gripped the window-sill tightly. Above the roar of the storm, Mum's voice floated up. 'Jack!' and then something else I couldn't quite hear.

I looked down. My eyes streamed, but I just managed to make out her pale, upturned face in the dark garden below – then *thwonk*, something heavy and soggy hit me in the face. I jerked away, but saw a coil of wet rope disappearing over the window ledge; just in time, I grabbed it. What on earth was she doing?

I held on to the rope and reached for one of the towels we'd piled on the bed. I wiped my face and noticed the torch which had been half-hidden by the towel. I snatched it up and went to the window again and shone it down into the garden.

The rope stretched away and there, at the end of it, I could make out our rowing boat. I realised it was bobbing about – floating on water where the garden had been. I looked around for somewhere to tie the rope, but could only think of the leg of the bed, so I lashed it to that. Then I shone the torch around everywhere, looking for Mum. But there was no sign of her. And all the time, the screaming of the storm filled the room.

'Mum!' I shrieked, but the wind grabbed the sound and tore it away. To my surprise, though, I heard an answering shout from downstairs, in the hall.

'It's all right, Jack! I'm coming!'

I ran out to the landing and gasped. Mum was already half way up the stairs, dripping wet; below her the hall was already swimming with water which seemed to be rising as I watched.

'Look at the water!' I shrieked.

Mum pushed wet strands of hair from her face and smiled at me. 'I *have* seen it, you know – I've just been *in* it!'

She stopped on the landing and slowly pulled off her boots, pouring water from them over the handrail to splash into the hall below. Then she peeled off her long, wet socks. Slapping wet footprints on the bare floorboards, she went into the bedroom with me following, every movement accompanied by the rustle of our waterproofs.

With the window open, a deafening roar filled the room. In a moment, Mum was across the room and managed to wrestle the window as closed as it could be, with a rope in the way.

'Pass me something – oh, one of Dad's belts, there, on the back of the chair,' she said, holding on to the window for dear life.

I grabbed a thin leather belt, and helped her tie it round the catches of the window. At last she could let go and now the window was only slightly ajar; and though it strained at the belt, the roaring of the storm was a lot more bearable. Mum dragged the curtains back across, and they billowed and fluttered like sails.

'Why did you tie the boat up – up here?' I asked, but she didn't answer. She was choosing things from the pile on the bed – fresh socks, the flask of water, biscuits, a fruit cake someone had given us at Christmas. From outside, I heard the strange, deep, thundering sound which was like the wind but wasn't the wind.

'What *is* that sound?' I asked.

'It's the sea,' said Mum, as Dad had said earlier, and now I understood what that meant. 'It has come, and it's still coming. Let's get into your room where the window is closed. It'll be warmer in there.'

A thought struck me.

'What about Dad? And . . . Mr and Mrs Downes?'

Through all this, Mum had been as calm as if

she had dealt with this situation many times, though, of course, she hadn't.

Now she looked at me and couldn't hide the worry behind her eyes.

'I'm sure they're all right,' she said bravely. 'And he'll probably see them safe and then come back for us. In the meantime, we just have to wait.'

I followed her into my bedroom and she dried her feet with towels and dragged on dry socks.

And then, all of a sudden, the lights went out. We clutched each other, plunged into pitchy darkness. The deep roaring grew louder, and the whole house seemed to shudder with us. The next moment, there came a crash of breaking glass downstairs, and the roaring was in the house, and inside us, shaking every cell in our bodies. I put my hands over my ears, but could not block it out. Now I had a memory of walking on the beach in rough weather, and realised that I recognised the sound – it was the thunder of huge waves, rumbling in and smashing on the shore, but much, much louder than I'd ever heard before.

3

Aunt May

'The torch,' Mum said suddenly, 'I'm sure I put it ready . . .'

Her voice, cutting through the darkness, dragged me out of the terror which was gripping me.

'In your room,' I said. 'I was using it.'

I felt her get to her feet from the floor next to me and I reached out and grabbed her leg. I didn't want to be left on my own.

'Hold on, I'm coming too,' I said, trying to sound as normal as I could.

Mum picked her way to where we thought the door was, and I could hear her patting the wall, then there was the clap of her palm against wood, and she had the door open. We felt our way along the landing, hugging the wall, hearing the rush and slap of water below us as if we were walking along a jetty. Then Mum gripped my arm a little tighter and pulled me through the doorway to their room, which was as dark as everywhere else. The wind whistled and snapped loudly at the part-open window, and it was much colder in here.

'I think I put it back on the bed,' I said, fumbling my way over, Mum still gripping my arm. I couldn't remember, and felt stupid. I hadn't understood the importance of the strange things Mum had pushed into my arms, but now I was starting to realise.

My shins told me I'd found the bed when I walked slap bang into it. I started to pat around the objects in the dark. It was like playing some silly game, and it wasn't the right time for it.

'I bet if I draw the curtains there might be a bit of light,' said Mum, hearing me grumbling under my breath. I heard the rustle of material, and then a soft light beamed through the windows. The glow fell far enough into the room to sprinkle itself coldly over objects on the bed. But as I started to pick over them, I heard her make a little sound of surprise, then: 'Got it! On the window-sill.'

She swung the beam over towards me.

'There,' she said, 'that's a bit better. Grab the bits of food, and the flask, and let's take them back to your room – it's warmer in there.'

'Shine the light on the bed again, then,' I answered. I wasn't at all hungry or thirsty, to be honest, as fear has a way of clamping up your throat and stomach.

I picked up as much as I could and passed her bits and pieces, then she led the way with the torch and we slipped out of the door to the landing again.

'Ugh!' said Mum suddenly, and stopped.

I nearly bumped into her.

'What is it?'

'I didn't put my wellies back on when I changed my socks and now I've trodden in a wet patch. Must've been where I dripped before . . .'

She shone the torch down at her feet and trailed off.

A small puddle had collected on the planks of the landing.

I was impatient. The flask was starting to slip

where I held it in the crook of my arm, and a packet of biscuits in each of my hands meant I couldn't do much about it.

'There are more socks in my room, Mum.'

But now I saw where she was directing the torch beam – past the edge of the landing. It lit up a moving sheet of water just below; the staircase had vanished entirely. As it slapped and boiled, drops flicked between the spindles in front of our feet, and that's what had caused the puddle.

'Oh!' said Mum. 'Oh, my goodness.'

We stood, frozen.

'Mum,' I said, a terrible thought coming into my head, 'Mum, is it still rising?'

'Shh,' she said, holding the torch beam on the water as if she felt that would hold it back. 'Give me a minute.'

Was she thinking the same thing as me? What was above us – the loft? There was no ladder to reach the hole; that was downstairs, outside, underwater. And what if we got into the loft, and sat there, in the musty, cobwebby dark with no way out, and the water rose even to there – what then?

'I should get my wellies from your room – I need something on my feet. Then I think it's best if we stay in my room, even though it's colder. Till we are sure it's going down again,' Mum said firmly.

'Whatever – I'm coming with you,' I said just as firmly.

We picked our way to my room, and I stood in the doorway while Mum grabbed her wellies, then we turned and splashed back to my parents' room again. Neither of us said it, but the puddle on the landing seemed bigger, even in that space of time.

I put the food back on the bed, and Mum hooked the torch up from the lampshade in the middle of the ceiling, where it swung in the draught from the window and swept crazy shadows around the room. Then she changed her wet socks for the second time, and squashed a towel inside her boots and rubbed and rubbed until they were dry enough to put on.

We sat on the bed and waited. The shaking of the walls and floor had stopped, but we could feel a steady humming through the bed, which I knew now was the rolling of the sea through the house.

From time to time, Mum gave me a hug and said things like: 'Rescuers will come soon. We just have to sit it out.'

And so we sat, staring at the floor, until we saw the water begin to trickle around our feet. I reached up to the dangling torch and pointed it at the door behind us; the light shimmered back at me from a steady stream sliding across the floor beneath it.

'It's coming in, Mum,' I said; though of course she knew that already.

'All right,' she said, getting to her feet. 'Time to get out.' She sounded defeated.

Baffled, I watched her pull back the curtains and start pulling at the leather belt we'd used to tie the window.

'Shine the torch this way, would you Jack?'

I pointed it so that she could see what she was doing; suddenly the window flew back and hit the wall outside, and I heard the glass shattering.

The wind screamed into the room and started to shake the door.

Mum jumped back, shocked; then, as if woken

from some dream, she grabbed the rope, and barked instructions at me. 'Get the torch and switch it off a minute to save energy. We can see enough at the window. Put the strap round your wrist. That's it. Now, help pull on the rope.'

I was glad I had gloves on. We hauled and hauled on the rope until coils fell on the bedroom floor. As we did so, I heard dull thuds and each one made the house shake. What on earth was it – and would the place collapse? Mum, who was in front of me, said suddenly: 'There she is! Bless her, dear old *Aunt May*.'

I looked out, and there she was, nudging the house wall eagerly, almost level with the window – our wooden dinghy, her mast empty of sail. *Aunt May* – so called because we'd bought her with money Aunt May had left us – had come to save us.

Mum didn't need to explain her plan. While she held the boat tight, I undid the knots at the leg of the bed, and started to pull up all the slack rope.

'Leave a bit of slack, though,' said Mum quietly, watching me. 'We don't know how much this water is going to rise. She needs to rise with it.'

I did as she said, then tied the knots again. Mum heaved on the rope so that *Aunt May* couldn't pull away from the house.

Then I went first – one leg out of the window, then the other, balancing for a moment on the window-sill. I looked down. The edge of the boat scraped against the bricks of the house, then swung away, leaving a gap filled with dark, glittering water. It was important not to fall into that gap, when I jumped. I managed to swing my heels so they hit the inside of the boat and kept her against the wall for a moment, then I pushed off and landed safely on the timber planking.

For a moment, I just felt relief. But now I really became aware of the dark violence of the storm as it screeched and swirled around me.

I looked up at the window for Mum, expecting her to follow, but first her hands appeared, full of the things we'd put on the beds. I took them from her, both of us working in silent haste. The sea beneath me rolled and heaved and I staggered to keep my balance. Standing upright, out here, the freezing wind attacked me mercilessly, and I felt I would turn to ice, despite all my clothes.

'Mum!' I called up when she was back at the window. 'It's so cold!'

She didn't answer, disappearing from the window so I wondered if she had heard me, but then I saw blankets dropping towards me and I pulled them away from the water just in time.

Now Mum's leg appeared over the sill, and then the other. With difficulty, she bundled her violin case out in front of her, and dropped it down to me. Then she readied herself to jump, while I did my best to keep *Aunt May*'s side close to the wall with the boat hook, but it was hard work with nothing much to catch on to.

Then Mum slithered down and was in next to me, the boat rocking wildly for a moment, and we grabbed each other and sat on the seat, pulling the blankets around us.

It was terrifying. Not just because of the danger of the storm, but because the whole world as I knew it had gone all upside down and crazy. It would be terrible to be out at sea in this, in a boat – but it wouldn't be so weird if you'd actually set out in one. It was something else to find yourself in a storm, on the sea, in your *garden*, when earlier you'd been minding your own business, safe and cosy in your house. Out on the wild ocean, sailors probably feared giant waves and swells or rocks; tied to the side of our own home, we suddenly saw new and bizarre dangers. The thumps I'd heard on the walls when I was inside were being made by all sorts of floating things smacking into the side of the building – things that should have been in people's gardens and houses. We cowered in *Aunt May* as they thudded near us, but most of the time the building made them ricochet off its corners and miss us. Here was a shed roof; now a fence panel; a bin; and then, the horrifying sight of a child's buggy with a lifeless body in it – but as we grasped at it, sobbing, and pulled it towards us, we found it was a just a child's plaything, with a dolly in it.

The saddest object was the chicken ark from three doors along – I held on to Mum to stop her falling in as she pushed it away from *Aunt May*'s flank, and tried not to look at the soggy, rust-and-white bundles of feathers floating within it. And all the while the wind screamed, and the rain stung and lashed our backs with ice and there was an eerie sound of splintering and groaning all around; but eerier than that was the lack of any human sound, no shouting, no crying – and no sounds of rescue.

And that was how we stayed, all night, as carts and trees and dead animals and roofs and entire small buildings floated past us.

4

Eighteen Months Later

Sometimes you know when the day is going to be special. You can just feel it.

But I have to admit, when I woke up on this particular morning, I didn't feel anything much – except sleepy. I sat up in bed and rubbed my eyes and yawned as usual. I pulled the edge of one curtain. White-gold light and heat came crashing at me through the open window – another scorching day in the making already, though it was still early. I let the curtain drop back to keep the room cooler and stumbled around, dragging on clothes.

I didn't hear the knock at the front door, because I was splashing in the bathroom. As I came out, Mum called up the stairs:

'Jack?'

I peered down at her from the landing.

'Hmm?'

There she stood in the hall, looking smaller than ever, far below me – hair short but wild, dressed, as usual, in men's overalls which had once been blue and were too big for her, and muddy boots. She had something in her hand – it looked like a book.

'That was Emily. She brought you this.'

I trotted down the stairs.

Mum passed me the book.

It was thick and homemade; the covers were of cardboard, covered with dull, greenish fabric which had been glued on. The pages were of different sorts of scrap paper by the look of it, cut to roughly the same size as each other and sewn together at the spine with waxed thread. They were crammed in, pushing the covers open if you didn't hold them together. Every page seemed to be covered with small, neat handwriting in different-coloured inks.

'She said it's from Michael,' Mum added.

'I know,' I said. 'It's one of his diaries. The latest one.'

I tried to press the covers together, but the top one pinged from under my thumb and pages sprang up beneath my face, covered in Michael's words and thoughts. This book was itching to be read. I was dying to read it. But not here or now, in snatches at the bottom of the stairs. This would be something to savour. First there was breakfast, and work to do.

Mum looked at me carefully.

'I have my boots on already. I'll deal with Van. The bread is fresh out of the oven. Get yourself breakfast. Today, you have a day off. You sit and read that book.'

Mum can be a slave-driver but she also has an amazing knack of knowing what's best, and possibly even mind-reading. I didn't put up much of an argument. I could feel the diary bulging like a flower bud about to pop. Nothing could stop that, or tell it to wait.

I put it on the side in the kitchen and set about cutting the bread while Mum went back outside to do my chores.

Then, with a cup of warm milk in my hand,

trying not to get bread, butter and jam on the pages, I sat at the old kitchen table and started to read.

<u>February 14th</u>

Valentine's Day, the calendar says – no cards for me and Em of course, big surprise – but not a bad day, all in all. Doctor came and said I'm over the worst with the latest chest infection, and that I can sit around in the wheelchair, but I'm not to try walking. For goodness' sake! Not much chance of getting up to anything with Em around – she was there, listening to him, eyeing me like a hawk.

Anyone who's got an older sister will understand. It's pretty horrifying ending up with them in total charge of you – can you imagine?! But then, when I was younger, I never guessed what the flu would do – ripping families apart, or taking the lot – really, we are lucky compared to some. At least we have each other. And it can't be exactly fun for poor old Em. She nursed our parents, she lost her fiancé, and now she's stuck looking after her crippled little brother.

Anyway, today was a bit exciting – well, in that something happened, for a change.

I was sitting in my seat by the window of the front room, where I am most days when I'm well enough. From there I can see down the drive and watch people going past. They can't see me very well, and mostly don't bother to even look towards the house. Stuff has grown all over it so I suppose, to them, it's starting to disappear.

One or two people know I sit there though, and look for me and wave to me specially. Tom, for example – I sat next to him when I went to school – used to drop in and chat a bit, but he does that less often now. I think, like a lot of people, he's realising I'm not going to get better and be back the way I was, so it's hard for him to see the point ... and of course, like everyone, he's busy. Then there's the man with the horse and cart, making deliveries and picking up other things to transport on his way out again. Don't even know his name. Haven't even spoken to him. But he sees me looking and always waves and smiles, always.

I love the sound of his coming ... the hooves on the road seem to thud in time with your heart. Then you hear the jingle of the buckles and bit and now you see the horse – ears pricked, white stripe down the middle of his face, sun shining on his coat, the colour of leaves in autumn; picking up his feet smartly, white sock on every leg – very handsome. He has to slow past our cottage to take the bend, and that's when the driver smiles and raises his hand to me, seeing me there at the window, and I wave back, even when I'm tired and it makes me ache even to do that.

Then they are past and gone and once more the day stretches into emptiness, with a clock ticking, and I am bored and fall in and out of sleep . . .

But today was different.

I heard the sound of not one but two horses and it wasn't even the right time for the carrier's horse and cart.

Two very big, bay horses came clopping around the corner, pulling a much bigger cart – a modern, covered wagon, no less.

'Em!' I called, wondering if she'd hear. I'm not sure sometimes if Em genuinely doesn't always hear me, or if she sometimes chooses not to. 'Come and see this!'

Em came in looking a bit grumpy and wiping her

hands on a tea towel. 'What is it? I'm trying to finish washing up— oh!'

She stared out of the window with me. The big, bay horses had stopped and were standing steaming in the cool air. There was foam around their mouths and they stamped impatiently.

'Well! I wonder where they are headed?' she said to me. 'Do you think they're lost? Should I go—'

'They're moving again,' I interrupted.

Slowly the wagon creaked into life, but only rolled a little way past our drive, then stopped again.

'Next door,' I said. 'But no one lives there any more. Why on earth . . . ?'

'I'm going to see,' said Em, and trotted away.

I got that feeling I always get at times like this; the urge to jump up and investigate with her, then a sinking feeling when I realise I can't any more, followed by a bit of frustration and envy — how could Em just leave me waiting like this and get all the fun herself? Then I feel guilty about those feelings, and try to be patient, and wait, and know that Em will hurry to tell me what's happening just as soon as she can.

Anyway, Em seemed to be gone ages, but I expect it

was really only minutes; then she came back saying: 'New people! Next door. Some of those east-coasters the government has had to evacuate. There's a boy. They look OK.'

I stopped reading suddenly.

The boy, I thought – that's me, Jack. Michael is writing about our arrival here. It felt odd reading what someone else had written about me – almost like prying or eavesdropping. And of course, this was a diary, which is usually private. But Michael had given it to me, so I knew it was all right.

I remember that day well. Cool but sunny. A strange feeling in the pit of my stomach which couldn't decide whether it was fear or excitement. The fear came from not knowing – oh, so many things. What would this part of the country be like? What would the house be like? What would we do once we got here?

But when we saw the transport – the massive, stamping horses and the huge covered wagon – and we were helping the men load it with *Aunt May* and our very few other possessions, I felt a strange thrill of excitement, which grew when we got on board and set off. The excitement seemed to swamp out the scared feeling, and I think Mum felt the same. It didn't help that we were almost ready to go before Dad turned up at last. He'd slipped away earlier to say goodbye to the Downes, who had managed to keep him for ages by reliving for the fifteenth time the whole terrible story of the night he rescued them, and of course, showering him with their undying gratitude.

Though Mum sniffed a few tears and Dad looked pale and serious, when we got up into the wagon and the horses took the first clopping steps away from the boarding house where we'd been staying, both of them gave each other and me big squeezes and smiles.

The journey had taken ages, with stops for the horses to be rested and then, later, changed for new ones. We drove out of the town, through villages, beneath the humming silver-white wings of wind turbines rooted across the sweeping plains; now past green-shaded growing tunnels which slowly opened and closed with the strength and journey of the sun like great, long, winking eyelids; now past fields full of green crops sprouting from terracing like the seating at football stadiums, except in lines, not an oval, and if you watched, the solar sensors made the top tiers lower to take a little shade and the next tiers rise up to enjoy the sun, and so on, all across the field, like the most amazing Mexican wave.

The swaying of the wagon kept sending me off to sleep, so that it seemed I was in a very long dream.

When we came at last to the village which would be our new home, Mum gave me a little shove and I sat up and looked out. We were travelling along a winding lane, edged with hedgerow, then low, old, stone walls. Small, golden cottages nestled up against each other. They looked like they'd been there for ever, grown out of the ground: paintwork cracked and peeling, mossy, crooked roof tiles, old-style solar panels. Then, as the lane drew us into the centre of the village, these were mixed up with taller, grander, old red-brick buildings, some with columns and porches before red, green or black front doors so shiny they reflected our wagon going past. Now came an ancient church, roses around the gateway, old headstones tilting with the land, and finally the cluster of traders and shops huddled in the centre – places and people I would become so familiar with, over time.

There was the tailor's and dressmaker's, with ready-made clothes in the window along with rolls of fabric, where we'd buy everything we wore, along with everyone else in the village – except for a few with fuel-cell cars. The shop was run by a very nice middle-aged couple called Mr and Mrs Prince, who were always dressed totally immaculately; the only odd thing being that though they were very friendly to everyone else and everyone liked them, they no longer spoke to each other. This could make things tricky in the shop sometimes, but all the villagers had got used to it. No one knew what they had argued about, long ago, and some people said they reckoned that even the Princes had forgotten by now.

Another sort of shop, looking more like a small barn, without windows, had a faded blue sign over it, reading *J. W. Acre – We Mend Everything*. We'd later call this 'the menders' like everyone else. The J stood for Josh, a small, grey-haired man of very few words, bundled up in striped wool and old tweed with holes and darns, who did, in fact, manage to fix anything you took there, from a broken teapot to a mobile phone. Next door, an almost identical sign announced *H. W. Acre* (we later found out this was Josh's brother Harry), *Wheelwright and Cartwright*. When I first went down to the menders to get something fixed for Mum, Josh wasn't in, but Harry came across to see what I wanted. I thought he was Josh, because he looked just the same, but discovered that he was chatty and spoke quickly, unlike Josh – so that's how I told them apart from then on.

Then the general store, with all the things you'd ever need: seeds, hairbrushes, soap, rope, bioplastic bags and containers, groceries for the old people who might no longer be able to make or grow things themselves, and special things like sugar and coffee and chocolate. This was run by two old ladies, Celia and Tamara, both white-haired, one stout, the other tiny and hunched, and I learned, like everyone else, to check my change carefully, and to watch the scales on the weighing machine, because they made mistakes which you might put down to their incredible old age: 'Oh dear me, I am sorry, young man, did I only give you sixty-five back? No, that is right. Oh, no it isn't, is it? You gave me this . . . I do get in a muddle. Here you are, then.'

My mum was given polite hints from a few neighbours that it was interesting that the ladies never got it wrong so that *they* were out of pocket. They would notice immediately if you gave them too little money, and had eyes like hawks' for a foreign coin handed to them by mistake, and if they weighed something wrong, it was also in their favour, so perhaps they weren't so ga-ga after all.

I didn't know all this, then, of course. And when we pulled up at the house which was to be our home, had I noticed Michael, sitting watching in his window? Later, he'd been such a familiar figure there, but no, on that day, I don't remember seeing him. I was just sort of aware that the house next door was swamped with climbing stuff and ours, though old and shabby, did at least look like someone might live there.

I wonder what they think of the place. The Blake family had kept it nice, till the flu took hold and they disappeared, one by one. That family had lived there for ever. Me and Sam Blake, we'd had a laugh — fishing, climbing, getting told off for coming home covered in mud and nettle stings . . . I try not to think of Sam. Anyway, won't take much to set the house right again! What sort of place did they come from? I hope they're not disappointed. And what did they do, where they came from? What will they do here?

Well, Michael, we weren't disappointed. Shabby it might have been, but all we saw was a lovely old cottage, somewhere the water would never come, and it was ours, and we were all together. We looked at each other as the driver helped us down, each of us instantly in love with it, but wondering what everyone else thought. Would Mum think it too small? Would Dad think it too shabby? Maybe *they* were thinking, Jack will think it's too quiet, too boring. So we didn't say anything for a moment, and the driver broke the silence first by saying: 'There now. Isn't that pretty? Just waiting for a family like you to love it a bit.'

'It's beautiful,' said Mum, smiling at him, and we all felt relieved, and Dad said, 'We're very lucky and very grateful,' and I think I just made a whooping sound and managed to get through the front door first, to start exploring.

We had wandered all over the inside, which didn't take long, as there were just two bedrooms and the bathroom upstairs and a front room, kitchen and sort of back porch which Mum called a utility room.

Then we went out of the back door and stared. The garden was a jungle, and it was hard to see where it stopped and started, but it was huge. It was more than just a garden. It was practically – well, a field.

'It's bigger than I thought,' said Dad.

'Surely this isn't all ours,' said Mum. 'Though if that's our turbine up the far end . . .?' She pointed, and you could just see the rotors peeking out of the tall pole which had been completely covered in bindweed.

They hugged each other and smiled.

'Plenty of room for everything – all the food we could ever want,' said Mum.

'And more than we need. Enough to trade,' added Dad happily.

So that's what our new life was going to be. That's what we were going to do.

5

The Carrier

<u>March 6th</u>

It's been quite interesting watching the work going on next door — certainly makes a change, something to look at. I have taken to sitting and looking out of the back bedroom window lately, because all the action is behind the house.

They have cleared all the bindweed. Great rambling vines of it ran over everything, including the wind turbine, hanging heart-shaped leaves and nodding big, white trumpet flowers in summer. Mum used to call them rainflowers. She was a bit superstitious — said it was supposed to rain if you picked one. But it's not true. We either have downpours or drought, it doesn't matter what you do, pick flowers or leave them.

Then they dug out brambles and nettles, rescued the hidden fruit trees and bushes and already they have vegetable beds with little green things growing in neat lines. It looks great. Today I watch the man and the woman digging and lifting; I can almost hear the bite of the spade in the damp soil, feel the wood of the handle in my palms, the heave of the muscles as the weight is lifted, turned. The woman pushes the hair out of her eyes, the man stops for a breather, puts his hand in the small of his back and leans on his spade for a moment, and I realise I can almost feel his tiredness, and I remember how it feels, but it's a good thing, made from burned energy.

My kind of tired is a weak, lazy kind of thing, made from having no energy in the first place. I wish I was out there helping. Maybe, when I'm better, I will be. I'm curious about the boy, of course. He works hard too. I don't know what's happened about school. I watched him set off in the mornings, at first. Now he seems to spend a lot of his time digging, weeding and planting — when he's not waiting for the carrier.

Because, like me, he seems to have a thing about the horse and cart. I was sitting one morning, waiting at the window, and there came the carrier, and I waved to the driver, who waved back as usual. But as I watched him pass, I saw the boy next door standing, staring too.

Next time, I glanced across as I waited, and sure enough there was the boy again, waiting out in front of his house. This time, the carrier didn't pass on by, but stopped. He chatted to the boy, who smiled at him and talked back while he stroked the horse's nose. The carrier hadn't brought anything for them – he seemed to pause just to say hello, because after a moment, with a click of his tongue, he was off again, along the road and out of sight.

I was surprised to find I felt – well, jealous. So I thought, if the weather is OK, then maybe Em will let me sit out when the carrier comes tomorrow, in my wheelchair. Then maybe I can pat the horse too. If that sounds pathetic, well, I'm sorry. Imagine my life. It's a big deal to me.

March 7th

Em fusses around and starts wrapping me with scarves and blankets. I am worried in case we end up missing the carrier. He comes at five past nine sharp and it's almost nine. 'Hurry up, Em,' I say. 'It's not that cold.' She pushes the wheelchair outside. She stops by the front door. 'No,' I say, 'I want to be right by the gate.'

'Why?' she asks. I haven't told her about wanting to stroke the horse; worse still, let's be honest, the reason behind it — mainly because I've seen the boy next door doing it. Em thinks I just want to be outside.

'I — I might see someone I know and I don't want to shout to talk to them,' I say.

'Oh,' is all Em says, and she pushes me a little further, to the gate, and kicks on the brakes. She is pretty nice, really, when she wants to be.

She goes back inside, and in a couple of moments I hear hooves coming up the lane. Slam goes next door's front door behind me, and then footsteps hurry along their path. I realise it's the boy, and now he's alongside me, at his gate.

I hadn't really thought of this. It's a bit embarrassing. I will have to say hello, of course. But before I can, he looks across and calls out, 'Hello! Are you waiting for the carrier too?'

'Um, yes,' I say. But the carrier isn't bringing me anything. Maybe the boy'll think I'm a bit odd — maybe the carrier will think that too. Just sitting here in a wheelchair to be closer to the horse. Maybe they won't stop. But next minute, the horse is here, rounding the corner, one ear pricked forward, one tilted back towards the driver, his coat splashed with sunshine I hadn't noticed before, and all thoughts go out of my head.

'Whoa!' calls the carrier, and takes in his reins, and the horse steadies and draws up smoothly, so his head is just at my gate. He stamps a front foot and plays with the bit in his mouth. The rings jingle, silver, flecked with foam. I am astonished by the size of him, close up. His head alone is as big as my middle. The driver's voice snaps me out of my staring.

'Hello, there!'

I look up and see a cheerful, lined face, with pale-blue eyes above a neat, trimmed grey beard.

'Hello,' I say, and follow with the weak wave I usually do from the window.

'They let you out at last, then.'

'What? Oh, yes. Been a bit better. Thought the air would do me good,' I say. My voice sounds squeaky, rusty like old gate hinges. I am wondering if I dare stroke the horse. I might have to lean out of the wheelchair.

'He's very handsome.' I try clearing my throat, and find my voice is better. 'Could I pat him?'

'Course you can. He's friendly enough. He likes the break, to be honest. This bio-fuel we're carrying today is pretty heavy. He's starting to stop here of his own accord now.' And the carrier nodded across to the boy, still waiting by his gate.

With difficulty I reach forward and grab the top of my gate. I will have to pull myself up to stand for a moment, which I don't do that much inside the house, and usually only with Em to help. It occurs to me that I haven't really thought this through.

'Hang on a sec,' comes the boy's voice, and he is through his gate like a shot. He rubs the horse's nose, pushes past him, and reaches over my gate for my hands.

'Ready?'

He gives a pull, and he's surprisingly strong. I am out of my chair – not quite upright, I admit, still a bit folded in the middle, but sort of standing – with the boy holding my wrists and my fingers clutching the gate.

'All right?' he asks, and now his face is close to mine. He has brown eyes and freckles and his hair is a bit of

47

a mess, but he is smiling in a friendly way. He doesn't look scared of me or anything. 'All right?' he asks again. 'I mean, do you feel safe for me to let go?'

'Yes, yes,' I answer, then add, 'Thanks.'

He nods and skips back out of the way so the horse's head and neck are there again, the other side of the gate. Slowly, I dare to take one hand off the gate. My legs sag a bit but take my weight. I reach out and stroke the horse along the neck. He is warm, incredibly so, and the hair is smooth as silk, the muscles beneath are hard as rock. A scent rises up from him – close your eyes, and it's like hay, leather, beer and burnt sugar.

I wish I could see the expression in the horse's eyes, but they are behind blinkers. Still, he seems OK. He stands quietly for a moment.

I reach behind me for the arm of the wheelchair with my hand and the boy is there again, in front of me, holding on to my other hand, so I can let go of the gate completely and sit down. My legs feel tired, even after those few seconds, but still – the blood races around my body and I feel alive.

'Well done, Jack,' says the driver, and looks at me as if expecting something, so I say, 'Yes, thank you – er,

Jack,' but both of them still look at me, so I add, 'I'm Michael Cox,' and this seems to be what they were waiting for, as they smile and the carrier says his name is Simon. Jack stands at the horse's head, rubbing the white blaze, which the horse likes almost too much, because it starts to rub back till it nearly lifts Jack off his feet. I realise that, for the moment at least, I am safer behind the gate.

I am a bit disappointed to hear the horse's name is Spud, and I think Jack is too — such a lovely-looking creature, and the carrier can't even remember why he's called that. And then he has to go, to get on with his deliveries — so with a creak of wheels and a slap of leather, they are off, and me and Jack are left at my gate, watching as he disappears down the lane.

Jack doesn't rush off. I try to think of something to say.

'Settling in all right?'

'Yes, thanks,' he says.

'Your mum and dad have been working hard,' I say, then wish I hadn't, in case it sounds like I have been spying. Nothing better for a poor invalid to do all day.

But Jack looks pleased.

'They have, haven't they? Looks a lot better now. We're going to grow veg and sell the surplus — well, we hope so.' He is climbing on his gate and swinging on it. Em would say that this will break the hinges, but I used to do it all the time, and our hinges seem OK, so I don't say anything.

'Not got school then?' I ask and again wish I hadn't. His smile disappears and he looks down at the ground.

'Well, I'm meant to,' he mumbles, 'but I didn't like it really. And we're so busy here and they don't seem to have noticed. It's only a sub-school. Half the time there are no teachers anyway.'

'That's not much good, is it?' I say quickly. 'Though come to think, I seem to remember there were some teachers who — well, it would've been great if they hadn't turned up.'

Jack flashes me a grin.

'Must get back in or Dad'll want to know why. They aren't happy about me missing school, but it's OK if I'm busy at home.'

'Of course,' I say. 'Bye.'

I hear his feet going away up his path as I sit, staring over the gate, down the lane.

Then I hear the footsteps pause and come back towards me.

'Michael?'

I can't turn round very well to see him, so I just say, 'Yes?' with my back to him.

'Are you OK sitting out here? Don't you want to go back inside, now the carrier's been?'

He seems to know that's the only reason I was out. I have a bit of a battle with my pride. I don't expect anyone else will pass for hours. It is getting a bit cold. And I don't know when Em will come to get me – she's probably trying to clear up and start getting lunch prepared.

'Well, it would be nice,' I say, trying to sound casual, 'but I'm not very good at wheeling this thing backwards up a slope. So I was just going to wait for my sister.'

'I'll do it,' says Jack, and just as I'm hesitating, dreading that he is sorry for me, he adds: 'You'll be getting me out of something much more boring anyway.'

So I say, 'Oh, OK then, thanks.' And he takes me back in the house. And before I know what's happening, Em has asked him round for lunch.

6

The Horse

I remembered that day all right – the day I first really got to meet Michael. But it was odd reading it from his point of view. I hadn't known then that Michael had been so ill and that trying to stand and pet the horse was a big step for him. I suppose I'd thought he was – well, that he'd always been like that. If I'd thought about it at all.

The school part made me squirm a bit.

We'd only just arrived, it seemed, when I'd been shunted off to the local sub-school. The main schools in towns were too far away for anyone outside of those towns to walk to, and only families with a transport business had a way to get their kids to them. So in villages everywhere there were sub-schools. Books and equipment, and sometimes teachers, were borrowed from the main schools for three or four mornings a week. They set you work which you were supposed to do at home the rest of the time. The main teachers were whoever they could find from the village – usually retired or not really qualified. So sub-schools had become a bit of a joke. My last one had been closed half the time on days when it was supposed to be open, because someone was ill or whatever, and I didn't suppose this one was going to be a lot different.

I turned up all right, at a shabby little building which had once been a community hall. It lived up to all my expectations. I shuffled in with very few other kids of all ages and met teacher number one.

Mr Butt.

He had a mop of too-long, curly hair which flew around over his eyes when he got excited, and which he'd then sweep back with wild gestures, like an actor. He was dressed almost entirely normally, except for a scarlet and blue cardigan which hurt your eyes. He thought himself young, which he wasn't, but maybe this was because teacher number two, Mr Hargreaves, was about eighty-nine at least.

Mr Butt stood in front of us as everyone talked,

and called out for quiet a few times, then tried clapping his hands. This worked for a moment. Then he spotted me.

'Ah! A newbie! Jack Crosby, isn't it? Nice to see you here,' as if I'd just dropped in by choice. 'I'm Mr Butt.'

The rest of the kids must have known his name by now, but it didn't stop an immediate giggle and lots of jokes bubbling out into a major racket within seconds.

I'd have felt quite sorry for him, and was quietly pleased that the class's attention wasn't on me after he'd singled me out like that, but I soon began to dislike him.

He clapped his hands together again and his hair flew over his eyes. He shoved it back and called out, 'Now, now, a bit of quiet. I don't see there's anything funny about the new pupil joining us.'

Ooh, desperate, sir. Two boys either side of me stared at me, luckily seeming to decide there wasn't in fact anything funny about me, and raised their eyebrows and smiled, one of them drawing an invisible circle in the air by his forehead to show me, in case I hadn't realised it, that the teacher was bonkers. But I felt a shove in my back and looked round and saw a boy with a face like a pig, scowling. 'You're weird,' the owner muttered between clenched teeth.

The older boy next to me shoved him back.

'Shut up, Fred Simpson. Weird yourself.'

Mr Butt tried to teach us some maths by doing sums on the board pretty much by himself; we were supposed to call out answers for him to fill in, but generally he seemed to prefer his own, so people let him get on with it after a while. Occasionally he got excited in the middle of a long sum and called out things like: '*Now* we're cooking – with *gas*!' leaping about the board as he did so, sweeping back his hair and stopping to stare somewhere above our heads with glittering eyes.

Still, at least he was lively. Teacher number two, Mr Hargreaves, wandered in, talked about grammar and spelling or history or geography (or whatever took his fancy, it seemed) in a loud, fluting voice which whistled down his nose, and wrote on the board, all without seeming to notice if anyone else was there. It was very odd. Kids chatted, got up and wandered about in or even out of the room, had a little scuffle, and he just carried on. We wondered if he came in and did his lessons in the same way on days we weren't there. But he did set work, and take in our books and mark them, and as he handed them back he would make a comment to the owner.

In my second week there, I queued to get my homework back.

Mr Hargreaves paused, looked at the cover of the book, and said, 'Oh, Jack Crosby. You're new, aren't you?' Without waiting for a reply, he went on with his loud, old-fashioned voice, 'Dear me, you should have said you couldn't read or write. All I can suggest is that you do the separate exercises I've set with your parents at home. I take it *they* can read and write?'

I felt my face turn scarlet.

'Yes,' I managed to blurt out.

A voice came from behind me. It was Fred Simpson.

'Told you he was weird; can't read nor write either,' and there were giggles and snorts.

I hardly heard Mr Hargreaves as I walked away, full of rage and shame.

'That's enough, Simpson. Hardly Einstein yourself, are you? You can take a detention tomorrow afternoon for that.'

This didn't make me feel any better, and I was right to be worried. The next time I went to school, a stone whistled past my ear as I was about to enter the hall, and later, Fred's older brother Jim spat so close to me it landed on my shoe.

I started to make excuses about going, and Mum and Dad, who knew about these sorts of schools and were too busy to make a fuss, didn't nag me much about it and said they'd do work with me at home. But like I said, we were busy.

Then, one morning, me and Dad were up on the roof, cleaning the solar panels. They were so filthy and green with algae they weren't trapping much sun, and we needed the power as the wind turbine wasn't enough on its own.

Mum called up from the back door of the kitchen below us.

'James? Someone from the village wants to ask you about his generator. Could you spare a moment?'

Dad clambered down the ladder with me after him, and at the bottom there was a middle-aged guy, a bit overweight and puffing, even though he was just standing there.

He held his hand out to Dad.

'Brian Simpson. Pleased to meet you. We live just a little ways down from you, below the village. I hear you're an engineer.'

Simpson, I thought, peering around in case he had one of his sons with him.

'Well,' said my dad, 'I'm a civil engineer, or I was. Flood defences. And before you say anything, mine held fast, I would like to add. I'm not a mechanic. You've problems with your generator?'

'It's just stopped, so we have nothing, no power at all. And there's no one in the village to fix that kind of thing now, since McCormack died. Josh Acre says he's up to his ears in work. I'd have to wait days for a visiting mechanic. Someone told me you might be the man.'

Brian Simpson looked a bit desperately at Dad and I felt sorry for him, in spite of Fred and everything. He didn't *look* horrible.

'I'll take a look at it, of course,' said Dad, 'but if it needs a new part we could be in trouble.'

Mum popped up behind us at the back door then, saw Mr Simpson's expression, and added, 'James can fix anything,' which made Dad shoot her a dark look over his shoulder as the two men headed for the side gate. Then he noticed me.

'Well, come on, Jack, why are you just standing there?' he said grumpily. 'You may as well come along and learn something, if you're not at school.'

Mr Simpson looked at me, puzzled, as I hung back, and then his face seemed to soften.

'My lot are, Lord help the school, so an extra pair of hands might come in handy. Come on, lad.'

So I wouldn't bump into Fred or Jim – I wondered if he'd made that clear on purpose.

We walked down the lane in the soft sunshine,

down a dirt track on the right, and soon came to a farm cottage. It was pretty clear from the smell that they kept pigs. To the right of the garden path there was a concrete yard, fenced off into pens, and the sun glinted off pink, ginger and black backs which just showed above the planking. But I hardly noticed, because I had just seen something entirely unexpected. A horse.

There he stood, in the last of the pens, head down, eyes half-closed, paying no attention to us at all.

Dad and Mr Simpson were disappearing around a corner of the house. They hadn't noticed me standing there, rooted to the path in surprise. I glanced after them, then turned and opened the gate to the yard. Inside the pens, the pigs squealed and grubbed through the muddy straw. When they spotted me some rushed up, others rushed away, and a few huge ones, sleeping on their massive sides like beached whales, did nothing but twitch an ear at the flies.

The horse opened his eyes a little more as I approached, but did not turn towards me. When I was close enough to get a good look at him, I stopped. He looked smaller than the carrier's horse, and it was hard to see what colour he was, as he was caked in dried mud. His lower legs and feet were hidden, sunk deep in mud, dung and filthy straw. Occasionally he swished his tail, which was so long it rested on the muddy bedding, but still the flies crawled all over him. One of his eyes was running so that the flies clustered there thickly. I reached up to brush them away, and he swung his head sharply away from my open palm.

'Sorry, sorry old boy. Just trying to help,' I said, putting my hand down again. When I spoke to him, he turned towards me for the first time, and even put his ears forward a little.

I reached out more slowly, keeping my hand low, and gently placed it on his neck. This time he didn't duck away, so I rubbed gently, feeling the crusty mud powdering off beneath my hand.

A soft patch of frosted red-chestnut hair gleamed where the mud had been; a strange colour for a horse, almost pink. Looking closely, I realised that this was because his coat was made up of white and red hairs growing together.

'Jack? Jack!' came Dad's voice from the path behind me.

I looked round to see him standing there.

'Coming!' I yelled back, and the horse jumped.

'Sorry,' I whispered again, and ran back to find Dad frowning.

'What the heck are you playing at? You're supposed to be with me. You can't just wander off around other people's properties. Anyway, you might get hurt.'

'There's a horse,' I said, following him around the back of the house. 'I was just looking.'

We'd reached an outhouse now, and Mr Simpson was fiddling with something inside, near the doorway.

'I don't care if there's a giraffe. Stick close by, would you?' grumbled Dad.

Mr Simpson looked up and smiled.

'Looking at the pigs, was he? They are pretty good, aren't they?'

'Yes,' I said politely, not sure what the difference was between a good and bad pig. 'And your horse is nice too,' though this wasn't entirely honest, as the carrier's horse was handsome, I knew, and the poor old thing in Mr Simpson's pig-pen was hardly in the same league.

'Oh, that! That's only there temporarily,' said Mr Simpson, passing an oily rag to my dad and stepping out of the way so he could get to whatever bit of the generator needed attention. 'I've got no permit for a horse – just the pigs, as they're for food.'

'Do you need a permit for a horse?' I asked.

'Crikey, yes. Otherwise everyone would have one, wouldn't they, for their own transport? Need a Methane Emissions Permit, same as for the pigs and cattle and sheep, and a Feeds Permit, which is tricky to get – you have to be using the animal for a carrier business and so forth. So it'll be gone within the week. Fellow owed me money and couldn't pay. The horse is worth nothing but I had no choice but to accept it instead.'

'Pass me the wrench, Jack,' said Dad, suddenly sticking his head out from the guts of the generator. I stared at the floor uselessly for a moment, then spotted the open toolbag and found the wrench. As I passed it to him, thoughts flew around my head. Mr Simpson talked about the horse like it was an old, broken piano or something. And how could it be worthless?

'Where is it going?' I asked, straightening up. 'Will you sell it?'

Mr Simpson laughed.

'I told you, it's worthless. The fellow I had it off would have sold it if anyone had wanted it. No, I'm afraid it's going in my freezer with the next batch of pigs. Horsemeat isn't as good as beef or venison, but at least it's something.'

'Oh,' I said, my heart jolting with shock at his words, then sinking. I thought of the carrier's horse, noble and proud, gleaming and full of life. When he was old and worn out, would he end up in a filthy pen, flicking at flies, for the last week of his life? Could you – *should* you – eat something like that?

Dad peered out. He had black smudges across his nose. He passed the wrench back to me.

'Small screwdriver, not the cross-headed one,'

he ordered, and as I searched in the toolbag he added to Mr Simpson, 'Venison! Now you're talking. We've got a deer trying to trash our vegetables. I keep hearing the government deer shooters behind the house, but they don't seem to get him. If I get hold of that it'll be venison, I'm telling you. But won't an old horse be a bit tough eating?'

I passed him the screwdriver; he gazed at it absently.

'Oh no, it's not old at all. Just a youngster – only four,' said Mr Simpson. 'It's not worthless because it's worn out. It would have been a good carrier's horse, but it won't be broken to harness, apparently. Badly injured someone who tried.'

'Oh,' said my dad, staring a bit longer at the screwdriver I'd given him.

'Is that the right one, Dad?' I asked. He looked at me as if he had no idea what I was talking about, then said suddenly, 'Yes, no, I mean, it is,' and stuck his head back inside the generator.

Not long after that, there was a splutter and a roar and the thing came to life, and Dad and Mr

Simpson patted each other on the back, and then did the same to me, though I had only passed tools, and me and Dad staggered down the path, our arms loaded with frozen bacon and pork chops and sausages.

I could just about see the muddy horse from above the packets stacked under my chin. I paused and called, 'Bye, horse.' He turned his head towards us.

Dad stopped too, and sighed.

'Shame,' was all he said.

7

Questions and Answers

<u>April 19th</u>

I get stronger and stronger. It's great. Yesterday, Em spotted Jack and his dad cleaning their solar panels and happened to mention to them that ours needed doing. I say 'happened to mention', but of course Em knew full well how the conversation would go. It went just the way she wanted, so today they were round here putting up the ladder, and I wasn't completely useless. I could manage to take a bucket of water from Em and pass it to them and stand out there watching.

Jack was half way up the ladder, taking it to his dad at the top, when he spilled some on my head. I gasped, Jack laughed, and his dad was just about to tell him off, when, without thinking, I grabbed a wet rag, chucked it at Jack and got him slap bang in the middle of his laughing face. Brilliant! Obviously haven't lost the magic touch – maybe I'll get the cricket stuff out and show him how good I am at bowling.

We laughed so much – even Jack's dad – that they nearly fell off the ladder and I almost called Em for my wheelchair. After that, Jack's dad said he would manage the last bit and I could entertain Jack, so we went off for a walk around our paddock.

Em passed me my stick, as I was still a bit shaky, and the paddock had become really rough and overgrown.

I showed Jack the place where the woodpeckers nested, and we looked hopefully in the far corner where I'd once found an adder, but there were no snakes today.

Then we dusted off the old wooden bench a bit, and I set up a piece of old board against a rock a few metres away, in front of the hedge. We hunted about for stones, then settled down on the bench with our ammo in a pile either side of us, to shoot at the target.

While we were keeping score and so on, Jack told me about the horse he'd come across at the Simpsons' place. As part of the story, it slowly came out about the school and Fred Simpson and his brother. I could see why he didn't want to go.

I interrupted him at this point.

'Hang on, don't throw for a moment. I'm going to get some of my stones back,' I said, and hauled myself off the bench and started gathering up the strays around the target.

I'd just picked up the last one when, 'That's one of mine,' said Jack, 'but thanks, I'll have it back.'

'Your eyesight must be pretty fantastic,' I muttered. 'Not to mention your memory.'

'I know it's mine because it's grey,' said Jack cheerfully.

'Unlike mine and all the others round here, I suppose,' I said, then added, 'Anyway, the Simpsons. I know them of course. Old man Brian isn't too bad, I suppose, but Fred and Jim . . . ! It's no good about the horse, though, is it? What do you plan to do?'

'What do you mean?' asked Jack, taking his precious stone from me.

'Well, I don't think he should just go in the freezer, do you?' I settled back on my seat and prepared to throw my stones again.

'Hold on, no friendly fire please,' said Jack, jumping to his feet. 'I'm going to get mine back now. I don't think Dad's too happy about the horse either. But he won't go in a harness and that's the only way you can get a permit for him. It is a shame though. I'd love to be like Simon. I could be a carrier.' He bent down to pick up a stone, so I couldn't see his expression, but I realised his voice sounded a bit choked.

'You could too,' I said. 'You've got a way with horses, haven't you?'

He straightened up and looked at me.

'Have I?'

'I reckon. You're quite comfortable with old Spud, at any rate.'

'Maybe – but even saying the horse did take to harness, there's nowhere to keep him. Our land is full of fruit and veg.' Jack sighed and rubbed the stones together in his hand.

'Have you finished? In which case, get out of the way or you'll have to be an unfortunate casualty – I'm two up on you at the moment and I intend to win.' I took aim with my stone to prove I was serious.

Jack skipped out of the way.

The stone whistled, and went thunk in the centre of the board.

'Ooh, lucky,' he said, sitting down next to me and selecting another stone.

'The horse could go here,' I said. 'Me and Em can't do fruit and veg. The place is too overgrown.'

Suddenly I realised what I'd said. It was true. I paused and stared at Jack and found him pausing and staring back. His brown eyes glittered. Time seemed to stand still as thoughts rushed through our heads.

'What would Em say?' he asked. 'And how would I get him from Simpson? I don't think Mum and Dad could afford to give away much veg in exchange and I doubt he'd want it anyway.'

'Em is always moaning about the grass getting out of control — she's scared it'll catch fire in the drought. But I'm not sure about how to pay for him — let's give it some thought. Talk to your mum and dad about it first.'

The sun was going down. We picked up and dropped our stones idly in their little piles, our game forgotten. Then we heard Jack's dad calling him.

'I'll do my best,' said Jack, getting up to go.

'Especially with your dad,' I reminded him as I got up too. 'He sounded like he was sorry for the horse, from what you say.'

His dad's voice came again through the lowering rays of sunshine.

'Coming!' Jack yelled.

He scampered ahead of me, back towards the cottage. Then he paused, and looked back.

'Michael?'

'Yes?'

'What if he won't break to harness?'

I stopped and shrugged at him. 'But what if he *does*?'

Jack stared at me and nodded slowly, smiling.

'See what you mean,' he said. 'Bye.' And he turned and was gone.

I set off again, feeling something was missing. It was only when I got to the back doorstep that I realised I'd left my stick at the bench. I'd walked all that way without it.

April 20th

I was down at the gate waiting for Simon the carrier at

least ten minutes early this morning. Really, I was itching to see Jack again and ask him how his mum and dad had reacted to our plan about the horse.

To my surprise, I was no sooner there than Jack and his dad came down their path together. His dad had a very serious expression on his face.

'Good morning,' he said.

'Good morning, Mr Crosby,' I said back.

'Please, call me James.'

I looked at Jack for clues, but his face gave nothing away.

'Jack tells me you are offering the use of your land for him to put a horse on,' continued Jack's dad.

'Yes,' I said. 'If he wants. It would do us a favour. We can't keep the grass down.'

'I see,' said Jack's dad. 'And Jack's idea is that he will train this animal to pull a cart, and we can transport our produce in it. He has had nothing to do with horses before. Have you?'

'Well, no,' I admitted. 'But I would say for Jack, he seems to have a way with them.'

'Oh, does he?' said Jack's dad. 'Well.' And then he seemed at a bit of a loss as to what to say next.

Jack looked at me. I looked at Jack. We both looked at Jack's dad again. After a moment, he said, 'I just wish I knew more — about horses, I mean. For instance, maybe they need more land than your paddock. Will he eat everything and then it'll be just one big mud bath in the rainy season? Does he need a stable? Where do we get a harness from — not to mention a cart? And Simpson was told he'd injured someone when they tried to train him — Val is a bit worried about that part. And how would I pay Simpson for him? And what if he doesn't break to harness?'

'Mmm,' I said. Me and Jack had thought of a couple of these questions ourselves; now Jack's dad had added quite a few more. Still, I saw hope in that he was even considering the idea. At that moment, the loud clop of hooves rang out on the road and we all turned as the carrier came around the corner.

Spud slowed up and came to a halt by my gate, as was his habit now. Simon pushed his hat back on his head and looked at us in surprise.

'Well, well!' he called out cheerfully. 'Quite a party! Good morning, Michael; morning, Jack; morning, sir.'

Perhaps because some kind of explanation seemed

to be required, Jack started to tell Simon the whole story. This was probably the most sensible thing we could have done.

'Hmm,' said Simon, scratching his beard. 'All right then. Let me see. I saw the horse you're talking about the other day and it's a wicked shame to waste him. It's worth a try, if you're careful, mind, Jack. Yes, Michael's land is enough. No, you don't need a stable, except for yourselves, to keep you dry and so on when you're dealing with the horse. *He* won't care either way — he's enough shelter from rain and flies with the hedge. Yes, Jack does have a way with horses, but he'll need a bit of help and advice — I can do that. Harness — I have an old set you're welcome to. You'll need to get a better one in time but it would do just to see if this horse is going to play the game. Cart — I know where you can buy one, but you don't need one to start training. You'll find out whether he's going to break by pulling an old tyre, a wooden pallet, something like that. Then you can worry about carts.'

Jack's dad looked a bit shell-shocked by this. I think he'd half hoped Simon's expert advice would be to abandon the whole idea. But he watched Jack rubbing

Spud's nose and reached out and patted the horse himself, looking very thoughtful.

'Thank you,' he said. 'Now the solar panels are working, I think the mobile's charged up. I could give Simpson a ring now and ask him to give the horse a stay of execution, in case he jumps the gun. Though I don't yet know what I can give him for the horse . . . Val gives violin lessons, but I have the feeling none of his family would really feel the need for those.'

Jack giggled. I knew he was imagining Fred or Jim playing the violin.

Simon pushed his hat down more firmly.

'Save your phone,' he said. 'I'm going past his place. I'll ask him for you, and I hope you come up with something. Must be getting on — see you!' And he clicked at Spud with his tongue and the horse moved on, reluctantly.

'Well,' I said, but before anyone could think of anything else to say, we heard gunshots ringing out from somewhere behind our field.

'It's the hunters again, doing the cull,' said Jack's dad. The deer were getting squeezed out with everyone using every spare bit of land. The moors where they lived were protected, but droughts in the summer and mud in the rainy season forced them to come down to the villages to look for food when their numbers got too high. Then the government sent hunters out to cull the strays damaging people's food crops.

Suddenly, Jack's mum appeared in the doorway of their cottage. Her hair, though short, still managed to look wild and slightly as if she'd had an electric shock.

'James! The deer — it's injured and it's in the artichoke patch!'

Jack and his dad turned and rushed up their path. I didn't wait to be invited. I slipped out of my gate and in through theirs, and followed them. We arrived at the vegetable patch just in time to see a beautiful stag slump to his knees then crash down to stretch on his side.

We watched in silence as the damp flanks rose and fell; rose and fell once more, for the last time. The dark red rust of his coat was no match for the spreading pool of scarlet beneath him.

Jack's mum sniffed: 'To think he doesn't get to see the rest of this lovely day,' and broke down into real tears.

Jack's dad, putting his arm around her, said: 'And he doesn't get another boiling summer of flies with nothing to eat; another winter of grazing disappearing underwater. There isn't room for everything any more, Val.'

Jack stared and wiped his nose with the back of his hand. It was sad, but — did none of them see what I saw?

'Mrs Crosby,' I said, clearing my throat, 'he was taking the food meant for your family. And Mr Crosby — James — you do know that anything shot or dying on your land, by law, is yours, I hope? To do with as you see fit.'

They all turned and looked at me.

They think I have no feelings, I thought. I should have waited and said something later.

'Venison,' said Jack's dad, turning to stare at the deer. 'Simpson said he'd rather have venison.'

8

It's the Horse

Somehow the stag's death seemed to have a purpose to it – it was as if getting the horse was meant to be. One life for another. Like Dad had said, there just wasn't room for everything on this planet any more. People had to have fewer children, use less of everything, work harder. He said in the old days, people had had pets. Now, most animals had to do more in life than be fed and stroked all day. The horse would have one last chance to show where he fitted.

Michael knew that a deer had to be cut up quickly once killed, so Dad used the precious mobile phone to call Simpson after all, and he was round like a shot, with his older son Jim, a big wooden handcart, bioplastic sacks, and a set of terrifyingly huge knives.

When I saw them at the front door I hung back,

but Jim caught sight of me. As Mr Simpson followed my dad through the house, Jim paused. 'You're taking the horse, then?' he sneered. 'It'll probably kill you and then it'll still go in the freezer.' And he drew his finger across his throat.

Mr Simpson must have had good hearing. He stopped suddenly and turned back, a dull red flush filling his face.

'What was that, Jim?'

Dad, who hadn't heard the exchange, looked back, puzzled.

'Nothing,' said Jim sulkily.

Mr Simpson looked past him to me, and I could see he was embarrassed.

'Take no notice,' he said. 'I like a lad to show a bit of pluck. And not be idle, unlike some I could name.' Here he threw a glance at Jim, then added to me: 'Be careful, and if you get nowhere, I'll take the horse back and deal with it myself. At least you tried.'

Jim looked thunderstruck.

'And *you*,' Mr Simpson continued, the colour growing strong again in his pale face, his finger wagging towards his son, 'I'll have a word with you later. And Fred. For now, that's enough. Get out here and help me butcher this deer.'

And they clomped off through the house and out of the back door.

I followed at a safe distance. Mum was in the kitchen. She rubbed my hair.

'I'm going to hide in here. Cup of tea, Jack?'

'Good idea,' I said, and we sat at the table, waiting, blowing on our tea and feeling strange about the whole business going on out there. Within two minutes, Dad was back.

'Is there enough in the pot for me?' he said.

'Sit down,' said Mum, rather seriously. 'I'll get you a cup.'

As all she might normally have said would have been something like: 'Yes, I think so,' I took a look at Dad. He was a strange, greenish-white colour and there was a clammy, sweaty look to his hair.

'You all right, Dad?' I asked, worried. 'You're not ill?'

'No, no. Should've got out of the way, that's all. Didn't realise it would be so . . . ugh. Don't go out there, Jack.'

Mum passed him the cup of tea she'd poured.

'I think me and Jack already realised that it wouldn't suit us.' She smiled.

We sipped in silence for a while. Dad had made biscuits which were on a plate in the middle of the table, but none of us felt like eating. After a bit, Dad said, 'That's better,' and put his cup down and sat back in his chair. His face had gone back to its normal colour.

'What was all that in the hall?' he asked me, eyes narrowed. 'Between Brian and Jim? What did the boy say to you?'

I shifted uncomfortably.

'Oh, nothing. Just said the horse was no good,' I muttered.

'Did you meet him at school?'

'Not exactly. Fred didn't seem to like me from day one, then he must have said something to Jim, and . . . he made it clear he felt the same.'

'Did you have a fight? Did someone hit you?' asked Mum.

'No, no,' I mumbled into my cup. 'Nothing happened.'

Luckily, we were interrupted by Mr Simpson tapping lightly on the open back door and putting his head around it.

'We'll be off now. Taken the bags round the side way. Afraid your artichoke bed won't be the same again for a while, though.'

Mum and Dad stood up.

'That's fine,' said Dad, and Mum added, 'Well, it all turns to fertiliser in the end, doesn't it?'

The horse, I thought. What about the horse?

As if he had read my mind, Mr Simpson said, 'Are you fixed to take the horse? Just want him next door?'

'Um – yes, yes,' said Dad. 'I hadn't thought of getting him here. I suppose we should lead him round. Do you have a bridle or whatever it is?'

'He's got the halter he came with. I can get Jim to lead him round if you like – I could do with my pen back. And of course, I've no permit.'

'Well, if you're sure. That would be very kind of you,' said Mum quickly. She knew me and Dad hadn't led a horse before. Then she looked worried. 'For that matter, *we* don't have a permit . . .'

'You can legally have him for a week without one, especially if he's supposed to be awaiting slaughter – that's what I did. After that, you'd still get away with it for a little while till some official notices. To be honest they're unlikely to spot him for a while in the Coxes' land – till he eats it down, that is,' he chuckled. 'Give us half an hour to get this stuff out of the way.' He paused and looked over his shoulder as if to check where Jim was. Then he edged a little further in the open doorway, revealing a horribly bloodstained apron across his middle, and lowered his voice:

'I'm sorry about my Jim, young Jack, I've had a word with him. Turns out it's really Fred's fault – seems like you and he kicked off on the wrong foot and he made it out to be more than it was to Jim.' He glanced towards Dad, then Mum, and added apologetically: 'Fact is, neither of 'em has been the same since my wife died . . . well, nothing has, matter of fact.'

Mum and Dad, of course, immediately made lots of sympathetic noises and assurances that no offence had been taken, while I cringed in my chair.

Then Mr Simpson and Jim were off with their load, and Mum went out to survey the artichoke bed and perhaps dig it over, and I asked Dad if I could go round to Michael's to tell him the horse was coming.

'Oh dear, yes,' said Dad. 'It's only polite. And you know something, a thought's just struck me. Any minute that thing is going to turn up and we're just going to plonk him in there. Are the hedges and fences sound? I mean, he could get out – anything could happen.'

He had a point. We both thought for a minute, and remembering the Coxes' plot – completely overgrown – it suddenly seemed likely there were holes and breaks in the boundaries. We looked at each other.

'Come on,' said Dad.

Em, Michael's sister, answered the door. Dad broke the news to her that the arrival of the horse was imminent. We'd never been entirely sure that she was going to be happy about this – it was one thing for someone to complain that the grass needed cutting, quite another for them to feel delighted about this sort of solution. To our surprise, her face lit up. She looked a lot like Michael, I noticed for the first time.

'Isn't it exciting? I'm sure this will do Michael the world of good ... he's pottering about out there now, checking everything's safe. Do you want to come through?'

'Of course,' Dad said to me as we walked through the house, 'Michael's a step ahead. We should have guessed.' We saw Michael's head peeking out from above a patch of nettles as we came out of the back door.

'Hello there!' he called out to us cheerfully. 'Thought I'd do a bit of a tour of the ranch to check it's all in order for the round-up.'

When we got to him, we found he had been whacking at the nettles with his stick, like an explorer in the jungle.

'Thrash them to bits and they give up and die, eventually,' he explained. 'My dad used to do it. It's easier than digging – the roots run deep and for a long way.'

'Don't I know it,' muttered Dad. 'Damn near

killed us, getting our patch straight.'

'Well, you have to keep doing it for a while for it to work,' said Michael, 'and you needed your patch clear quickly. I've been around the boundaries, there are a couple of places where I could see a gap. Wasn't too bad though.'

We followed him and he poked his stick here and there to show what he thought were weak points.

'Nothing major. All a bit small for him to squeeze through, I'd have thought,' said Dad, inspecting the boundary. 'Though the gap in the fence here is a bit of a worry. If there was just something we could put across it . . .'

He stood up and we all looked around. The Coxes' land was full of old bits and pieces. Before we could do anything, Michael was away and heaving at a big section of board, half trapped by weeds.

Dad, shocked, sprang into action.

'It's all right, Michael, hold on a minute there, I've got it,' he said, seizing one end of the board.

I went to take Michael's end, but he grinned at me and shook his head.

'It's fine, I can manage.'

I shot Dad a look. I could hardly wrestle Michael for it, could I? Both of us, I think, felt awkward about hurting his pride. I watched with difficulty as Dad and Michael struggled with the board over to the fence, and propped it across the gap.

Then they stood back and gasped a bit.

I picked up Michael's stick and passed it to him. He didn't look too bad, surprisingly, only puffing about as much as Dad.

'Well,' said Dad. 'If he really wanted to get out, I expect he could, but let's hope he just enjoys all this grazing.'

Mum unexpectedly put her head over the fence.

'So that's where you got to. I hope you've checked there's nothing sharp or dangerous for him in there.'

We all looked at each other.

'Didn't notice anything,' said Michael.' Just an old bath he might fall over. But hopefully he has eyes.'

'An old bath?' said Mum, laughing. 'Got a plug for it? That'll be just the thing for his water.'

'Water!' I said, horrified. 'I completely forgot that!'

'What a good idea. I'll ask Em if she has a spare plug anywhere,' said Michael.

Dad shook his head at me.

'You won't forget water in a hurry when the hot season comes,' he said. 'It'll take quite a bit of work keeping him topped up. You'll have to carry buckets.'

'But you can use the bore-hole,' said Michael, surprised. 'Didn't you know? It's on our property, but it's for your side too.' He nodded towards our garden. 'The Blakes paid for half of the cost when it was put in. Me and Em manage pretty well on just the rainwater tanks.'

Mum and Dad stared at him and then at each other.

'Well!' said Mum. 'Thank goodness for that! It was going to be hard watering the plot and keeping the house in water just from rainfall. Still, we'll be careful with it all the same.' She strained to see over the fence. 'Where's the bath? Oh yes, over there. Trouble is, you'll lose a lot to evaporation in the drought months. But if you drag it into the shade under the trees, it'll get full of leaves and bits.'

I was relieved she wasn't suggesting that – it looked pretty heavy. I didn't fancy dragging it anywhere.

'It's got the shade from the fence to keep it cooler, where it is,' said Dad.

'We'll get a lid for it,' said Michael. 'We'll find something. We'll take it off at set times for the horse to drink.'

At that moment, Em called from the back door of the house.

'Michael! Jack! Mr Crosby! It's the horse!'

April 20th continued

So as they were telephoning Simpson, I realised I'd made an offer of a field and the horse might turn up very soon. I got back in and told Em. 'The thing is, Em, a field – people generally expect that to mean enclosed on all sides. Do you think it could get out?'

Em wasn't that helpful at first. 'Oh, I do love horses,'

she sighed, rolling up her eyes, I supposed, judging by the direction, to some imaginary flying unicorn.

'It'll make a mess, you realise,' I reminded her. I didn't want to put her off, but I needed to get her back to earth.

'Mmm,' she said vaguely. 'Why don't you check the fence and hedge if you're worried? Melissa, my friend at school – you remember – she had two. The little fat pony used to get out sometimes, she said, but I think that was because it was little. I suppose they squeeze through things. The big horse didn't. Seemed very quiet.'

I was pleased Em suggested I should check for gaps. Not long ago she'd have fussed and clucked around me if I even threatened to try and stand up. So I went and pushed my way through the grass. Early on, I heard sawing sounds and the chatter of men, and I looked over the fence. There was Simpson and Jim, his son, hacking away at the deer already. I saw Jack's dad put his hand over his mouth and totter off towards the house.

By the time Jack and his dad appeared round ours, I had found a few gaps and dealt with most of them by breaking bits of branch in the hedge and weaving them together, like Dad had shown me. I was pretty relieved that it looked OK when they arrived. They seemed impressed – maybe they had thought they would have to do everything.

We got part of the old chicken-hut roof and put it across the last gap in the fence – I admit I needed a bit of help with that.

It seemed we'd no sooner finished than Em was calling that the horse had arrived. Until then, it had all seemed a bit of a game – but when we went to the front, there was a very solid, very real and, it has to be said, very dirty horse standing at the door with Jim Simpson at the other end of his filthy, knotted rope.

The horse looked a bit surprised and so did Jim. I realised we made quite a welcoming committee. There was me and Em, and Jack and his dad, and his mum, who had just hurried around. We all stared; the horse looked uncomfortable and gazed around for a moment, then broke the silence with a loud sigh.

Jack's mum laughed.

'He says, is this *it*?' and she reached forward and stroked his nose. 'Sorry, old boy, did you expect a top racing stable?' and everyone chuckled, even Jim Simpson.

'Wait till he sees the grazing,' said Jack happily.

'Do you want him round the back?' asked Jim, and there was a slight pause. Everyone who knew remembered that Jim and Jack had issues between them.

'Er, yes,' said Jack, as he realised no one else was going to answer for him.

'Here you go then,' said Jim, and passed him the rope.

Jack paused again, then took it from him.

He'd never led a horse, I knew. He was planning to train it, to work with it. This was the first big step.

We stood back as he walked towards the side path and I let out a sigh of relief as the horse simply followed him without question, clop, clop, clop.

We came through the patch of garden behind then then Jack's dad overtook them and opened the little gate to the field. Through they went, then they stopped and the horse gazed around for a moment. Then his head went down and he started to rip at the grass.

Jack grinned at us and we gave little cheers.

'He seems to think it's OK, then.' He smiled. 'I suppose I should take off the rope . . .' and he reached down to fiddle with it.

Jim stepped forward. Once again, because he had to talk directly to Jack, he sounded awkward.

'It's all one — the rope and the halter. Just one piece of rope, knotted like. You'll have to take it all off. Better to anyway, in case he gets it caught up in anything.'

Jack pulled vaguely at the halter. The horse took no notice and carried on eating. Jim strode across.

'Like this,' he said, catching the rope where it passed behind the horse's ears and simply pulling it forwards and down over the nose.

'Oh,' said Jack. 'I see.'

We stood watching for a while longer, but the horse didn't buck or gallop about in his newfound freedom. He stayed where he was, eating the grass around his feet. Once he'd dealt with that, he took a step forward and carried on munching.

'Well,' said Jack's mum. 'That's lovely. Now we'll have to see about water in the bath.'

'I've a plug somewhere,' said Em. 'And it would be nice to get him cleaner — I wonder if there's some kind of brush . . .' and she and Jack's mum went off towards the house.

Jim wandered back towards us and shut the gate

after him. Then he leaned on the fence with me and Jack's dad, watching as the horse stepped slowly away, Jack resting one hand gently on his shoulder, in no rush to leave him. The steady sound of tearing grass and muffled chewing filled the air. Somewhere, a blackbird sang his clear, straight tune.

'I'm supposed to say sorry,' said Jim suddenly, to no one in particular.

'What for?' asked Jack's dad, surprised.

'My dad said I had to,' answered Jim, looking down awkwardly at his hands resting on the fence.

'No, I mean, what do you have to be sorry about?' Jack's dad tried again.

'It's like this,' Jim blurted. 'Fred is a right liar. He came home from school and had to go back in the afternoon for a detention. Dad asked why. He doesn't half get cross when that happens, because he needs us to help with the pigs. So Fred tried to make out your Jack got him in trouble. So I wasn't very nice to Jack. Then my dad got wind of it and took Fred by the ear to Mr Hargreaves and the truth came out. Your Jack did nothing against Fred – or me. So I've to say sorry.'

'Well,' said Jack's dad. 'Sounds like a

misunderstanding, that's all. If it makes you feel better, Jack didn't say anything to us about it. But if you need to say sorry, I think you have to say it to him, not me.'

'I know,' said Jim. 'It's just hard — I mean, what to say—'

I interrupted.

'How about what you just told us?' I said. 'And don't be too hard on Fred — he probably lied because he was scared. Get angry with a dog because you call and it won't come back to you, then hit it when it finally does — it isn't going to come back to you again, is it?'

Jim looked at me, perplexed.

'I mean, if Fred *had* told the truth about the detention, would your dad have been pleased with him, or angry? Do you see? It's safer for him to lie,' I tried.

'That isn't a manly thing to do, though,' said Jim. 'It's like what a coward would do. He shouldn't have done it. And he shouldn't have picked on Jack in the first place. Just 'cause Jack can't read nor write. Like Teacher said, Fred's pretty dim himself.'

At that moment, Jack's mum appeared with the plug for the bath in her hand. I don't know what she'd heard so far, but she stopped dead to listen. Jack's dad didn't seem to notice. He was cross and surprised.

'What do you mean, Jack can't read or write? Of course he can! He's had problems, sure, but—'

I groaned inwardly, but luckily, at that point, Jack's mum cut in.

'Jim, your dad – he's a good man. People think so, in general, don't they?'

Jim stared back at me, surprised.

'Well, yes.'

'Yes,' I added for good measure. 'Their family's been around as long as ours, for ever. My dad would always count on the Simpsons if he needed a favour, and we'd do likewise for them. Honest and fair. I'm sure Fred is too, generally.'

Jack's mum was still looking at Jim.

'You want to be like him, yes? You want Fred to be like him? Your dad wants you and Fred to be like him?'

'Well, yes, but . . .' Jim shrank and looked down at his hands again.

'Fred's just a boy, not a man. Going round frightening and bullying him, or anyone else, telling him he's stupid, isn't going to make him turn into your dad. And it isn't going to make you turn into your dad, either. Anyone could tell you why he picked on Jack. Make Fred feel he's stupid and he's going to try and find someone to take his place as *most* stupid. Bully him and he's going to pass it on, to make himself feel bigger and better. And that teacher wants talking to as well. He should never have said that Fred was dim.'

We all stared at her in amazement.

After a moment, Jim cleared his throat.

'But Fred *isn't* very bright, to be fair, nice though it is of you to say . . .' he tried.

'Maybe not at school, he isn't,' Jack's mum continued, 'but he'll be bright enough to carry on with your business, with you to help him, won't he?'

'Yes, I suppose so. He does work hard, when you tell him what to do,' said Jim. 'And even Dad's said, he can pick out a pig that's ailing before we notice.'

'Then maybe Michael's right about easing up on him,' she said gently. 'Perhaps you should make more of what he's good at and be a bit kinder to him. Make it easier for him to be honest and tell the truth. I know you've both lost your mum. That must be hard for you, Jim, but Fred's even younger than you. Where does the kindness come from now?'

'Mmm,' said Jim, lowering his head and folding his shoulders even more.

'Anyway.' She smiled brightly. 'Go on. Go and make it up with Jack.'

He nodded and walked away across the grass to the boy and horse.

I sighed.

'Well, we've tried, Michael,' she said, rubbing my arm affectionately. 'But it can't be all down to Jim. He's only young and he's got his dad on his back too. I think I'm going to have a little word with Mr Simpson.'

'Good idea,' I said. 'He might listen to you.'

Jack's dad was still staring into the distance, as if he didn't hear us.

'Can't read or write? Hah!'

I looked at Jack's mum and dad, and sighed again. Who was going to have a little word with *them*, I wondered.

9

Van

It still seems odd, reading Michael's thoughts and words like this. The same events happening to both of us, but there he was, the whole time, seeing something me and my parents were trying not to. It makes me squirm, a bit.

While Michael, my parents and Jim were having their conversation, I was with the horse. He ate, and ate, and moved one step forward, slowly, as he finished each patch around his feet. I leaned on his warm shoulder and watched. The grinding of his teeth buzzed through his body, his shoulder blade, and through my arm, setting up a steady hum inside me. The sweet smell of broken grass scented the air I breathed. Dainty transparent flies, like fairies, floated up as he disturbed each tussock. Whatever my worries had been about how I'd cope, I knew one thing – I was very content here, with the horse, like this, and that was something, for now.

The next day, though, meant facing the truth. The horse needed a permit, and to get it he had to be in work. Nice as it would be to stand for ever at the side of him as he ate or to brush his coat till it gleamed, we had to get on with training – and quickly. We had a week to see if there was any hope.

I was up early, before the carrier came, and went round to Michael's, slipping into the side path and through the gate into the field without ringing the door bell, in case he wasn't up.

Nothing terrible had happened in the night. There was the horse, near the hedge, switching away the early morning midges with his tail. I picked up the rope halter and walked to the bath to check the water we'd poured in hadn't leaked out. It was still full. I rescued a couple of ladybirds with my fingertips, then headed for the horse.

He was dozing with his hind foot propped, but he pricked up his ears as I came over. I rubbed his nose and he blew hot air in my face and then sniffed around my pockets. Perhaps I should bring a treat next time, I thought.

I looked at the halter in my hand. It just seemed like a mess of rope. How on earth did it go on his head?

I untwisted it a little and decided to stretch it out and sort of imagine a horse's head in it. That worked. There was a round loop where the lead rope joined on, which would fit round his nose, and a longer loop off that, which would probably fit the length of his head.

I moved slowly, remembering how he'd ducked that first day I met him, as if he had been hit. I got the long loop behind his ears but then couldn't get the other over his nose. I started again, putting the nose loop on first, and this time it worked. The horse gazed at me patiently throughout. When I'd finished he gave his slight sigh again, as if to say, 'About time.'

I didn't have much idea of what to do next, but I supposed we might take a walk around the field as I needed to practise leading. We set off OK, the horse seeming tired and walking very slowly, but every so often he would stop and reach down for grass as if he were bored, and pulling his head up was like trying to pull a tree out by the roots. After a struggle, he'd lift it again and we walked on slowly. In that fashion we got to the gate, and there was Michael, leaning on it and smiling.

'Morning. Likes his food, doesn't he?'

'Mmm,' I answered. 'I don't know how to stop him. I mean, he's heavy and stronger than me. I can't lift his head. He just does it himself after I pull at him for a long time. My arm kills.'

'It's probably all in the training,' said Michael comfortingly. 'Like dogs. They can pull you over, can't they? Just have to learn not to. Are you bringing him out to see Simon?'

'I hadn't thought,' I answered. 'But I would like some tips. I don't suppose Simon can just leave his cart to come and see him. But would the horses be all right together?'

'Dunno,' said Michael. 'I could ask Simon and you could hang on here. He'll be here any second. Listen out for me shouting.' And he turned and headed off round the side of the house, really quite quickly. I noticed he wasn't using his stick. I hadn't counted on Michael to be a lot of use, but then, I hadn't realised he was getting better.

I let the horse graze while I waited. I didn't need anyone to tell me Simon had arrived, it turned out. For no apparent reason, the horse suddenly lifted his head, went stiff all over, and pricked his ears, staring in the direction Michael had gone.

'It's all right,' I told him, but he paid no attention to me at all. I patted his neck, and found it taut and trembling. Then, even I could hear the clatter of hooves outside, and with that, the horse lifted his top lip and gave an ear-splitting neigh. His whole body shook with it.

I gripped the rope tight and stared at him. The mud-covered, broken-down, tired horse had changed in a second. His nostrils flared, showing blood-red inside. The veins stood out on his face and neck. His body seemed to be made of muscle, moulded from metal like a statue. He was a charger in an old painting.

'Steady, steady,' I tried, and kept up a rhythmic stroking of his neck. I had no idea if it was having an effect, because he seemed to act as if I wasn't there, but I didn't know what else to do. I had a horrible feeling he was about to rear and leap about like those chargers in the paintings. Maybe he would jump the gate – then I'd have to let go – and what would Simon and Spud think when a wild horse bolted up to them and their cart?

Luckily, at that moment I heard feet approaching and there was Michael and, behind him, the carrier.

'Well, well!' called Simon. 'You got him after all.'

He didn't seem at all bothered by the horse's trembling and snorting, so perhaps it didn't mean much after all. I relaxed a bit.

'What about your horse?' I called back. 'Is he tied up or something?'

'No, no,' said Simon, reaching the gate. 'He'll just stand when I drop the reins. Trained. Has to be. Otherwise, how would I load and unload and so on? Let's have a look at him, then.'

He stepped through and the horse was polite enough to lower his head and accept a pat.

'He was very quiet before you came. I was trying

to lead him around. He was very slow, really,' I said. 'I don't know why he got like this when he heard you coming.'

'Oh, he's all right,' said Simon. 'Just lonely. Horses mustn't be alone, by nature. In the wild, they'd be dead without a herd. They stick together – lots of eyes and ears, strength in numbers, you see. He's been dumped in Simpson's pen for a week and now here, without another horse, and he's unhappy. Minute he heard another horse he got excited, that's all.'

'Oh,' said Michael, worried, from behind him. 'Do you have to keep two at a time, then?'

'Don't worry about that. He can have other friends, besides horses. They get used to a lot. No stables in the wild, are there, but my Spud goes in his stable all the time, like lots of horses. Spud's not as lucky for grazing as yours, though, I tell you. Turn him around in a circle for me, would you Jack?'

I pulled at the horse, and we managed a kind of circle, though he half trod on my foot once and tried to put his head down to eat and then threw it up when he heard Spud move out the front, and banged into me in his hurry to go back towards the gate.

I was breathless when I faced Michael and Simon again.

'How do you stop them doing – all that?' Michael asked Simon.

'You're doing very well, Jack,' Simon said to me, 'but he's a powerful animal. So is a little pony, for that matter. You want something more on his head than a bit of old rope, and then he needs to learn to take you seriously. Hasn't got any respect for you yet. It'll come. Just do what you're doing, be kind, don't shout and flap, but stick on with what you asked him to do till he does it. If he rams his shoulder into you, ram him back. Remember he's designed for other horses to bang into, that's what his mum would do if she wanted him to move out of the way, so you pushing him won't hurt him.'

'True enough,' I said. 'He feels like he's made of cast iron. But I reckon his mum was a bit bigger and stronger than me. I don't think he means some of it, he just hardly knows I'm there.'

'Ah,' said Simon, 'but look at his side – there – do you see it?'

I looked to where he was pointing.

A tremor flickered along the horse's flank in a sort of wave. A fly sprang off, settled again, and the skin twitched again.

'Cast iron, yes, but sensitive. He can feel that little fly through his hair. So remember that. Sometimes it's better to prod him with your fingertip than try to lean on him and shove him, if you don't want him standing on your foot.'

I let the horse graze again, thankful that he didn't seem to want to jump the gate or do anything else silly to get to Spud.

'What do you think of him, though?' I asked Simon. 'I mean, in general? He's not as big as Spud. Will he pull a cart?'

Simon looked surprised, stood back, and squinted at the horse.

'He *is* as tall as Spud. Fifteen hands or thereabouts. Maybe you think he's small because he's half starved. You did realise that?'

I stared at the horse.

'No, I didn't.'

'Well, brush the mud off him and you'll see the ribs. That's why his head looks too big for his body. Needs filling out all over. As for whether he can pull a cart, even a Shetland pony can do that. What sort of load? Well, I call the big heavy horses, like Shires, the lorries of the horse world; your horse and Spud, they're like vans. He'll be really useful – plenty of power for what you need. As long as he can be broken to harness, of course.'

'Half starved. Poor thing!' said Michael.

'You won't believe how quickly he'll improve,' said Simon calmly. 'The weight. That runny eye. The coat. Dr Green, they call it, the miracle worker. Grass, I mean. You've plenty of it. He's very poor at the moment and that's why he's slow and weak – but for you, trying to cope with leading and training, maybe it's a bit of a help. He'll get stronger and better as you learn to cope and get him under control. Now, I've got to get off. But I've brought you my spare old headcollar – I'll just run and fetch it.' And he turned and was gone.

Me and Michael stared at the horse.

'I suppose no one bothered feeding him when he didn't look like he was going to work,' I said.

'No – and no permit, no feed allowance,' said Michael. 'And not everyone has acres of grass. Oh well, he'll be all right here. You thought of a name for him yet?'

I had thought about it. But, though I didn't think much of Spud's name, any grander ones I'd thought of sounded silly when I imagined the muddy, tired horse. I explained this to Michael just as Em appeared.

'Well, I think you have to imagine him how he will be,' she said. 'I've thought of one, anyway.'

Michael looked at her, amused.

'Go on then Em, what is it? Mystical Dancer? Starlight Wonder?'

She sniffed and ignored him.

'Noble, powerful, handsome,' she said to me. 'Like Van Damme. That's a good name, isn't it?'

'Well, yes,' I admitted, partly to be nice to make up for Michael, who was now snorting. 'It sounds – strong. What does it mean?'

Em looked scandalised.

'Jean-Claude Van Damme,' she said. 'He was a great film star. Way back. Very handsome.' She stared away dreamily.

'Tough-guy movies,' added Michael. 'Good fights, though.'

'I don't mind Van Damme,' I said, as Simon reappeared.

'What's that?' he asked. 'For a name?'

'Em's idea,' said Michael, grinning.

Simon chuckled.

'Van for short,' he said, 'because that's what he'll be. Your van. You can call him the rest of his name when he steps on your toes.' And he and Michael seemed to find this very funny, while I looked over at Em and said, 'Thanks, Em, it's a fine name.'

'No problem, Jack,' she said with dignity. 'I'll find a photo of him somewhere. What's that Simon's got?'

'A headcollar,' Simon answered, coming through the gate to show me. 'See, it's real leather. It's got an extra strap going under his cheeks to get a bit more hold of the head – the halter you have

111

will come off too easily if you have a battle. This buckle on the side here is for getting it on and off. Plus, here's the real joy – there's a little chain here which runs under the groove of his chin. It sends a clear message he can feel better when he pulls you too much, or you want him to stop – otherwise you are just dragging on his nose. You clip the lead rope to it like this.'

He held the headcollar up while he was talking and though it was obviously old, it looked very nice – much more sturdy than knotted rope – but I still didn't really understand what went where.

'I'll put it on to show you once, then I have to go,' he said. 'So when you take it off, try and notice where everything goes, so you can get it back on next time on your own.'

'OK,' I said, gulping, and watched very closely as he put it on. To give him credit, Michael stared intently as well, so I knew he was going to try and help if I struggled next time.

'It's tempting to just take the rope off and leave him out in the field with it on. Some people do that, especially if their horse is hard to catch, but I don't advise it, in case he ever got hooked up in something,' said Simon. He hovered by the gate as I thanked him and set off to lead Van in a circle. The difference was amazing. Van lifted his head at a gentle pull of the rope and walked quietly along next to me, stopping when I did, never even trying to put his head down. He looked content, too.

'Oh, I'm glad I stopped for that,' said Simon. 'Much better. He's a nice colour, by the way. Wouldn't be surprised if he didn't have some Ardennes blood in him. They are good horses.'

'What – what colour would you call it?' I asked him. 'I've never seen anything like it before. When I first saw the white hairs mixed in with the red, I thought it might be because he was old.'

'Strawberry roan, or bay roan, some people call it. Looks like he has bay ears under that mud. I must be off. Keep at it and I'll call by again in a few days. Till then, keep practising the leading.'

'I will!' I called. 'Thanks, Simon,' and Michael and Em followed him down the side path to say goodbye.

I looked at Van.

'Right,' I said. 'A bit more leading around, then maybe you should carry on with the eating. Enough learning for now.' For Van, maybe – but Michael had other ideas for me. I see that now.

10

New Steps

<u>April 24th</u>

Jack has been doing very well with the horse, or Van, as he's now known. He has been leading him around the field and after talking to Simon, he took him out yesterday to check he was safe along the roads. After all, that is where he will be working.

Jack's dad walked along with him in case Van wanted to run away for some reason – Simon had warned him that horses can sometimes do that at bits of litter fluttering in a hedge, a bird flapping out of a bush or a dog jumping up and barking. I stood and watched them go, from the gate. I am feeling much fitter now, but I didn't want to go with them. I felt a bit strange about following. As I waited for them to come back, I realised that it's because I haven't been out of that gate for such a long time – well, I've popped next door, but not down the lane.

Funny, that, because Van simply stopped when they first led him into the lane and after a bit of chivvying he walked on quietly, then stopped again further along. Eventually they disappeared from view, and after what seemed like hours — but was only about twenty minutes — they came back. Van was stepping out quite smartly now, and every so often I could see Jack's dad put out a hand and give a pull on the headcollar to help steady him. When Jack told Simon today how Van had behaved, Simon explained that Van was nervous about leaving home — that was why he'd stopped a few times at first. And then, of course, when he was heading back — eager for safety and a familiar place — he'd started to hurry.

'They all do it a bit,' said Simon. 'And it's reasonable when Van is new here — he's probably worried you're going to take him somewhere else to live! But you must watch it doesn't become a habit — it's called napping. Walk out confidently and briskly when you're going away from home, so he feels he is with a leader, the head of the herd. Don't give him time to worry. Then always go a little slowly as you get close to home, on the way back. Otherwise he might rush or even bolt one day. If you do it regularly, it'll become a normal part of routine for him and not scary at all. In fact, he'll look forward to his trips out.'

This, of course, made me think about myself. Being ill, I'd not been able to go out, and I'd realised yesterday that it had now become a new and scary thing for me to think of wandering through the gate. Time to put two plans into action.

So, tucking a pen and paper in my pocket, and taking my stick for added safety, I opened the gate this morning and walked, just a few yards down the lane. The air felt good and fresh, flowers were starting to bloom in the verge. I paused at the corner where the lane divided into two, looked down over the village and admired the view. Then I turned slowly and made my way back to the gate again. It was nothing, but my heart rose in my chest, at first with the tingle of fear, and then, when the gateway was in sight, with a strange feeling of triumph. A little every day, I thought, and a little further every day.

Just as I got through the gate, the clatter of hooves announced Simon and Spud's arrival.

'Hello there, Michael,' Simon called out. 'Where have you been off to?'

'Just practising in case I start napping.' I smiled at him. 'It's been a while since I set foot outside this gate.'

Simon smiled and nodded.

'It's good to see you up and about. Is young Jack around? I have something for him. He'll need to get bit of a move on, if he wants that permit. After it's sent for, someone will come and check the horse is a *working* animal. So I brought him my spare old harness.'

'Oh good, he will be pleased. He'll be here any minute, he's expecting you.' I looked over my shoulder but there was no sign of Jack yet. I moved closer to Simon and lowered my voice.

'Simon – about the permit. When Jack comes . . .' At that moment, I heard a footfall and just managed to add: 'Play along with me, would you?'

Simon darted a puzzled glance at me but nodded, then called: 'Jack! How's it going?'

Jack arrived, out of breath, and reached out to pat Spud.

'Hi Simon. Hi Michael. Going very well. He doesn't seem frightened of anything. We went past a man shaking out a bag and a woodpigeon clattered out of a bush – it made *me* jump, but not Van!' And he grinned.

'Brilliant,' said Simon, 'but you've the hardest and most dangerous part to come. I've brought the harness. Here's a little book which tells you how to do everything — it's old, but that doesn't matter. Same rules, nothing changes.' And he passed over a small, dog-eared paperback to Jack.

'Oh, thanks so much, Simon,' said Jack, barely glancing at the book but looking beyond Simon to the harness, which was behind him on the driver's seat.

'I'll take a look at the book, Jack, and give you a hand,' I said, taking it from him. Simon jumped from the cart and pulled down a great quantity of leather and webbing, jingly metal rings and buckles.

I helped gather it up and somehow we passed it to Jack. He looked slightly alarmed.

'Bit more than a headcollar,' I said to him. 'You're going to need that book, aren't you, to sort this lot out?'

'Mmm,' he said. 'And you, Michael, to help. You could read bits out from the book while I try and fit it on.'

'Of course,' I said. 'Now, just stick it over there for a moment, Jack. We need to ask Simon about this permit.'

When Jack had put the harness into a big heap by the garden wall, I said to Simon, who had climbed back up to his seat, 'Our week will soon be up and Em has pointed out that as the horse is on our land, we are the ones who should get the permit sorted out. Where do we get it from?'

'You're right. Get the application sent off, and in the meanwhile, let's hope he becomes a working horse. I can give you the address to write to.'

I drew the pen and paper from my pocket.

'That's handy,' said Simon.

'Always carry them, just in case,' I lied. Then I fumbled, and dropped the pen.

Jack scuttled after it and picked it up.

'Thanks, Jack. I'm afraid my hands are still a bit shaky. Would you mind — could you take down the address?' And I passed him the piece of paper. I saw his face turn red, then suddenly pale, and I felt terrible. It's all for his good, I reminded myself. Jack took the paper and held it and the pen towards Simon.

'Perhaps you'd like to?' he tried.

From behind Jack, I managed to shake my head at Simon. He caught sight of me and did very well.

'Ooh, no, lad – my hands are full of reins and I've my gloves on. You do it – lean on the wall over there.'

'But . . .' said Jack, then, running out of excuses, went to the wall and smoothed the paper out nervously.

'You ready, son?' called Simon, and Jack nodded hopelessly. Once more, I felt rotten.

'Department of Farming – you can put Dept. for Department if you like – Transport and Livestock Permits . . . got that so far?'

Jack nodded, writing slowly. Simon winked at me.

'Peasington Street – Peas, like the ones you eat, plus i-n-g, then t-o-n . . . all right?'

'Peasington Street . . . yes, go on,' said Jack after a moment, concentrating furiously.

'Telford. Don't know the post code, but that'll get there.'

Jack looked up. He was still pale, and his eyes looked a little scared, but he was doing his best to put a brave face on it. He folded the paper quickly and stuffed it into his pocket.

'That's it. That's fine. Thanks, Simon.'

'Good luck. See you again soon. Make sure you follow

the book and you shouldn't come to any harm.'

And with a click of the tongue, Spud sprang into action and they were off.

We watched them go, then I said: 'I'll have Em write for the permit if you like.'

'Oh, would you?' asked Jack. 'Brilliant. I was going to ask Dad to do it, but he's so busy, he might forget.'

'Give us the address, then,' I said casually, holding out my hand for the paper.

Jack's face fell.

'Oh. Well, my writing's not . . . I don't think you'll be able to read it back.' He pulled out the paper slowly and started to smooth it out.

'Can you read it back?' I asked.

'Not — not that well. But I memorised the address anyway. I'm good at that,' said Jack, smiling faintly.

'Let's have a look. I bet I can read it,' I said, and now he didn't have much choice. He handed over the paper. I gazed at it. I kept my face very calm and still. There, on the paper, lay Jack's big secret. A spidery, wandering scribble. Because I had heard the address, I could just about make out what it was supposed to say. Almost every word was misspelled.

'That's fine. You do make a fuss, Jack. Of course I can read it.'

'Can you?' he asked, surprised and relieved. 'Really?'

'Really. Why would I say I could if I couldn't?'

Jack lowered his head and scraped at a stone on the ground with the toe of his shoe.

'At school, they said I couldn't read or write,' he almost whispered.

'Well, if you couldn't read or write you wouldn't be able to do this, would you?' I said, exasperated. 'Your writing is a bit hard to read, and a few spellings are wrong, but you can write. If you couldn't write, you'd be like a baby or a toddler, wouldn't you, just scribbling?'

'Yes – yes, I suppose so,' said Jack, looking up again.

'I don't know about your reading, of course, but I'm not sure anyone can write if they can't read, at least a bit. So I suppose you can do that too.'

'Yes – well, as long as it's not too hard, and only slowly,' agreed Jack. 'Everyone else is much better. The trouble is, if you can only read or write *a bit*, it isn't much use. Like only being able to swim a bit – a couple of strokes. Might as well not be able to do it at all.'

I grinned at him. Surprised, he grinned back. 'What?' he asked. 'What's so funny?'

'You are silly,' I said to him. 'I get what you mean. But if I fell in the river near the edge, being able to swim a couple of strokes would definitely be some use, compared to not being able to swim at all.'

'Hmm,' he said. 'Near the edge, maybe. Still reckon you'd probably drown.'

We turned and started to gather up the harness.

'*Probably* is better than *definitely*,' I bickered back. 'And anyway, how do you get better at swimming?'

'Practice. Doing it again and again,' said Jack, passing me a loop of reins. 'I can swim all right. Lived by the sea.'

'So it's the same with the writing and reading,' I reasoned. We began to walk up our path, Jack pretty well wrapped up in harness and me picking up parts that trailed.

'But I did practise that. Just didn't get better,' said Jack.

'Some things people get better at when they're older; it's just what suits them. I couldn't ride a bike when everyone else learned to, but I tried again a

124

couple of years later and I could then. Anyway, you haven't practised as much as the kids at school. I mean, you've hardly been going. That's weeks they've had that you haven't.'

'Aww! But they were already better than me.'

'What about before you came here? Or were you practising your swimming instead of going to school?'

'I did miss school a lot when we moved around when I was little,' said Jack.

'There you are then,' I puffed as we went around the side entrance. 'I am right, and you are wrong. Repeat after me . . .'

Jack giggled. 'All right, Michael. Whatever you say. Where are we putting this stuff, for now?'

'Um — the shed? Just here, on the right. What's that in your hand?'

'Looks like a brush. It was all caught up in the harness.'

'Oh dear. Think Simon is trying to tell us something?'

At that moment, Em appeared.

'What is Simon trying to tell you? Good grief, what is all that?'

'It's harness,' said Jack, 'and — er, a brush. I

hope Simon meant to give it us. It sort of came with everything.'

'I'm not *surprised* if he's trying to tell you something. I can't believe you haven't at least tried to get the mud off that animal yet. I could have lent you a scrubbing brush or something. If he's going to be a proper transport horse, he must look the part. Besides, it can't be hygienic — and to think, he was in a pig pen!' Em looked scandalised.

'You're right,' said Jack. 'It can't help with the flies, either. I'll get on to it right now.'

I was flicking through the little book Simon had given us.

'Says here make sure there's no sweat or mud on the horse every time you put on the tack. Otherwise it can rub and get sore.'

'Tack?' asked Jack.

'Harness, it means,' I explained. 'So cleaning him up is not just for him to look pretty. You will need to do that before we can go any further.'

To cut a long story short, Jack, feeling guilty, caught Van and tied him up to the fence. He started to brush, while I read out helpful snippets from the book.

'Start at the head end so the dirt flies away, work down the neck, then along the body towards the tail ...'

'Makes sense,' said Em, watching. 'Like cleaning a house. Otherwise you'll brush dirt on where you've already cleaned. Oh, he likes you doing his head, doesn't he?'

Van was closing his eyes as Jack brushed the mud from his fringe. As the grooming continued and Van seemed to like it more and more, Em disappeared into the house and came back with a small scrubbing brush. Unable to resist, she started on the other side of Van. The sun came out, the mud and dust flew.

'That's it,' I called out cheerfully. 'Keep going — it says here, apply firm pressure, regular strokes.'

Em and Jack paused and looked at me. Van was starting to look much cleaner, while they, unfortunately, were getting hotter and dirtier.

'Michael, useful comments only or I swear I'm going to chuck this brush at your head,' said Em.

'I only wish I could help,' I said, 'but I think two of you are enough. He's starting to look fabulous,' I added, to cheer them up.

It was true. By the time they had finished, there

stood in front of us a very different horse. His frosted pinkish coat gleamed, darkening at his head to a rich chestnut; his ears had black tips, and his lower legs were black, with one white sock; his mane and tail turned out to be black with white streaks running through. Em and Jack stood back.

'Wow,' said Jack.

'Goodness, he's handsome,' said Em. 'Like something from a fairy tale, or a circus. I told you he would be.'

'He looks somehow bigger,' I said. 'I know it sounds silly, but he's not a million miles away from how Spud looks now.'

'He's even better than Spud,' said Jack proudly. 'And it'll be amazing when he gets more weight on. Simon told us when we cleaned him up we'd see he was underweight. Look — there are ribs showing here and there.' He pointed.

'Mm,' said Em, 'and his hips stick out so you can see them. Spud is nice and rounded at the rear end. Poor old Van.'

'Shall I try and put the harness on now?' asked Jack wearily.

'Cold drinks first, I think,' I said sympathetically.

'And we don't want to rush things. Simon told us to follow the book. I've been looking through and there's some training we haven't done yet – very sensible ideas. Maybe the person who tried before didn't have this book and that's why it all went wrong.'

'I'll get the drinks, Em,' said Jack. 'You've been a real help. In fact, your side looks better than mine.'

At the kitchen table, sipping our drinks, we studied the book. Well, me and Em leaned over it and I pushed it towards Jack every so often to show him pictures and read the text to him with my finger following the words.

'It says *lunge* the horse – that's when you make it go round you in a circle at the end of a long rope – or lead it—'

'I think we'd better just lead him,' said Jack hurriedly, looking at the picture. 'What's that going round behind its back legs?' he added.

'I was getting to that. You get a long rope – we could use the harness reins – and rub them around the horse's back and hind end so it's not frightened. Then you let them drape around the back legs and lead the horse around. It says here it is natural for a horse to kick at things like that because it fears getting entangled or being attacked. But you don't want it doing that with a cart. So you start by doing this.'

'Mmm,' said Em. 'We need to be very careful not to get kicked. But I can't imagine it. Van seems such a nice, quiet horse so far.'

I nodded.

'But something went wrong once before.'

'Yes,' said Jack, putting down his glass, 'but like you said, maybe someone rushed his training. The book shows you that all sorts could go wrong if you do that. We'll do it nice and slow and see what Van is worried about.' He stood up, eager.

'I'm coming to watch,' said Em. 'You must be careful though, Jack. Do you think your dad should come and help?'

'No,' I said firmly, before Jack could answer. 'I think Van will be fine. I'll help Jack.'

11

The Mob

My mum put her head over the fence as we were
sorting through the harness on the ground.

'My goodness. I saw Van standing there and I
thought it was a new horse. Isn't he something,
now he's clean?'

'Simon gave us a brush,' I told her. 'And
Em helped.'

'What are you doing? Is that the harness? Are
you going to try him in it?'

'Maybe tomorrow, at this rate. We've got a book
and it says to get him used to the feel of the reins
around his sides and rear end first. I'm just trying
to get these reins off the harness.'

Mum laughed.

'Looks complicated. Are you sure you'll ever get
them all back together again if you do that? Why
not try a bit of the hemp rope we used to tie up the

luggage when we moved? It's pretty heavy and strong.'

I looked at Michael.

'Makes sense,' he said. 'If we undo all these buckles we'll only have to do them back up again tomorrow.'

Mum disappeared and a moment later she was back, passing a long coil of rope over the fence.

'Can I see the book?' she asked. Michael passed it to her and she read, frowning. I felt her looking at me as I sidled up to Van with the rope.

'Jack,' she said, 'I've read this and it sounds like you do the same as with a child – make sure he trusts you. Don't act like you've got a snake or a bomb in your hands! He's looking at you suspiciously already. Just do stuff like you know what you're doing, even if you don't. Act calm; you are not frightened of the rope, so why should he be? Imagine if I'd sneaked up on you like that the first time I tried to put a coat on you.'

Em and Michael stood at Van's head, where he was tied to the fence, and rubbed his nose and talked to him. I tried to act like Mum said. It was true – I certainly wasn't frightened of a bit of old rope, nor was I really frightened of what Van would do. I started whistling and, holding the coiled rope, rubbed it over Van's shoulder as if I was grooming him.

That went OK, so I flicked the rope loose and started to drape it around his back end. This time, Van turned his head, trying to see.

'I'm going to untie him, if you can hold on a minute,' said Michael. 'I'll hold him but let him see what you're doing. All right?'

No one said anything. I think we were all worried about Michael getting knocked over if something went wrong, but no one had the nerve to say it.

So Michael climbed over the fence and untied Van and I flapped the rope around a bit and let it dangle by his back legs.

'That seems all right,' called Mum from the fence. 'Now, it has a picture here, and the rope seems to go from the headcollar – except they have a bridle – and round his back legs above the bendy bits – do you call those knees? – but it goes through a strap around his middle along the way. Could you do that with the rope?'

'Hocks,' said Michael, 'that's what you call the bendy bits. Don't put the rope below them or he might step through it. I'll make a belt for his middle – pass us the rope.'

Michael, ever-prepared, took out his trusty knife and had soon cut off a length of rope and tied it around Van, behind his front legs. Em passed him bailer twine and he made two loops, tying one each side of the strap to pass the rope through. Then we made long reins from the rope that was left, which ran from the headcollar and hung in a loop behind his back legs.

Van stood very patiently while all this was going on.

'Like a professional film star with all the make-up and costume people around him,' said Em, whose main job seemed to be stroking his nose.

'Right,' I said. 'Now let's see what happens when I lead him around.'

'He'll be all right,' said Michael confidently, then ruined the effect by adding: 'But if he isn't, just let go. Can't come to much harm in the field.'

I turned Van away from the fence and led him further into the field. He walked normally for a couple of steps, then snorted and bounced forward, dragging me by the arm. Then he turned his head and stared behind him.

'He just felt the rope tapping on his back legs,' called Mum. 'Keep going! Whistle again! Don't act like you notice anything wrong.'

I gripped the rope a little tighter and, whistling, stepped out like we always did on our walks. Van walked after me. 'Silly horse,' I prattled to him. 'No snakes. No cowboys. No lions. Just an old bit of rope. Silly horse.' I carried on like this as we walked, and Van didn't bounce forward again. We did a circuit of the field and by the time we got back to where the others were waiting at the fence, he almost looked bored.

'Brilliant!' said Em.

'He was fine once he knew what it was,' added Michael.

We decided that was enough for one day, and I pulled off our bits of rope and the headcollar. A happy feeling swelled in my chest. It was all going so smoothly.

That afternoon, I sat with Michael on the bench we used for target practice, and we talked over how it was all going with Van. While we were talking, Michael dragged a bit of old stick through the loose, sandy soil. M-i-c-h-a-e-l, he wrote. Then he scrubbed it out and passed me the stick. 'My name's better than yours, unless you write yours where mine was,' he explained, sounding about five years old.

'Oh,' I said. 'Well, obviously Michael is a terrible name, Jack is much better. Here.' And I scrawled my name in the sand, j-a-c-k.

'Everyone has a capital letter at the start of their name. Shows you're important. So you aren't as important as me, then?' And he grinned and gave me a shove.

I gave him a shove back, brushed away the 'j' carefully, and made it a capital.

'There. Happy now?'

'Easier to spell than my name,' he said.

'True,' I replied. 'You have that "a" and "e" thing. How do you remember that?'

'Well, it's my name. I suppose it's one of the first things I learned to write. Can you spell it, now it's gone?'

I thought for a bit, almost put the 'e' before the 'a', then remembered and got it right.

'Very good,' said Michael. 'You don't seem to mind writing like this.'

'It's only names,' I said. 'And it gets scrubbed out. No one is going to see it.'

'Charming,' said Michael. 'I'm no one, am I?'

'I mean, no one like a teacher. Or someone at school. *You* won't laugh at it.'

'You know what your trouble is?' said Michael. 'You've got upset because people have been rude about your efforts so far. It's just the same as skateboarding. I've seen you, you're pretty good. But when you started, and fell off all the time, did people laugh at you? If they do, you either ignore them, laugh with them and get back on, or practise at home till you can face them.'

'That's the one,' I said. 'That last option. That's what I did.'

'Well, do the same with writing. You either

need to grow a thicker skin or you need to write in private.'

'But you can't write in private at school.'

'But you don't go to school, really, do you, at the moment?'

There was no answer to this because we both knew it was true.

'So, while you're not there, practise where no one can see, till you get better. Screw up the paper afterwards. I write every day. Well, almost.'

'Do you?' I looked at him, surprised. 'What for?'

'My diary. Not every day, because some days are just so boring I leave them blank.'

'Why do you write a diary?' I asked.

'I can't remember how it started. I think a teacher suggested it long ago, to – well, probably to make my writing better, now I come to think! I've kept one on and off ever since. Then I throw most of them away.'

'That seems a waste,' I said, 'but I suppose you don't want people reading them.'

'I don't really mind. I think most people would find them a bit boring, though. Do you want to see?'

'OK,' I said. I'd told Michael I wasn't a great reader, but I wanted to be polite.

Inside his cottage, on a bookshelf, there were rows of homemade little books. Michael pulled one out.

'Hmm. Last year's. Really dull. But take a look if you like.'

I glanced inside.

He was right – it was full of little comments about Em nagging him about not eating enough, or a robin visiting the window-sill, but the writing was clear and easy to read and looked really smart. I suddenly felt more ashamed of my scrawl, and of the fact he'd seen it.

'I wish I could write like that,' I said.

'Take that old one home, and copy bits,' said Michael.

'What?'

'Copy bits,' he repeated. 'That's how I got that handwriting. It's not really mine. I liked the teacher's so I just copied it. You can do that, can't you?'

'Well – yes.' I thought, if I see a cartoon drawing

139

I like, I copy it until I can draw it again later without looking at the original one, so maybe I can do the same for Michael's writing.

Suddenly, there was the sound of people shouting and many running feet somewhere outside.

We hurried to the front door and I ran down the path. I heard our front door open a moment later and Dad arrived at our gate at about the same moment I got through Michael's and into the lane.

There, in front of us, in the middle of the lane, was the local ambulance, completely surrounded by angry people. Women were standing and shouting, men were climbing on the bonnet and banging the windows. Several pulled at the doors, trying to get them open, but they wouldn't budge.

'What's going on?' yelled Dad, but with all the shouting no one paid any attention. I could just make out the driver and some other faces in the vehicle – a woman, I thought, and maybe some kids.

Now Michael and Em were behind me and Mum had rushed to Dad's side. A tall, hefty man who had been pulling at the handle of one of the doors suddenly let go and walked off purposefully. He was back after a moment with what looked like a pickaxe. Now the ambulance was starting to rock, side to side. I realised the crowd had organised itself – people were taking hold and trying to tip it over.

'No, no!' shouted Mum. 'He's going to smash the windows!' And the man with the pickaxe was raising the handle over his head, aiming for the windscreen.

Dad rushed forward, but someone else had got there in the nick of time – a hand grabbed the other end of the pickaxe, stopping the swing, and the hefty man turned in anger and snarled.

'What are you playing at, Simpson? Let go!' And then Dad was in amongst them, helping Mr Simpson by grabbing the man from behind and trying to pull his hands from the weapon.

'What on earth?' said Michael, next to me. 'Are they mad?'

'Oh, where are the police when you need them?' said Em. 'Shall I call them?'

At least the wrestling match between the man with the pickaxe, Simpson and my dad seemed to distract the rest of the crowd, so that they stopped trying to tip the ambulance over. Brian Simpson now had hold of the pickaxe and I noticed Jim for the first time, as his dad passed the weapon to him.

'That's *my* ambulance, Howard, mine and my family's for when we have need. I paid my taxes for this ambulance!' Brian Simpson shouted at the thickset man, his face almost purple with rage.

'Looks like he's going to need it in a minute,' said Michael. 'He's fit to have a heart attack.'

We moved a little closer. My dad had let go of the man's arms. Mr Simpson's anger seemed to have beaten even the crowd's rage, so everyone was quiet for a moment. But then a woman shouted: 'But we don't pay our taxes for the likes of them to take holidays . . .' and then the rest of what she said was lost as other people started shouting again.

Dad put up his hands in a pleading gesture.

'Please, all of you, stop it! Can someone just explain?'

But no one took any notice – everyone was shouting and waving fingers in Brian Simpson's face. At least for the moment they seemed to have forgotten the people inside the ambulance. I could see them now, more clearly. A terrified-looking man and his wife. Two little kids, crying, had pushed themselves through from the back of the van into the driver's section.

Suddenly, the shouting died down again, and a small figure at the centre of the crowd around Brian Simpson and my dad caught everyone's attention. I looked, and looked again. Michael, leaning on his stick. I couldn't believe it. I checked beside me, but he had gone. I had never noticed.

Em, the other side of me, caught my stare. She was biting her lip anxiously.

'What – what is he *doing*?' I asked.

'Lord knows. Trying to get some sense out of them, I suppose. He can never leave well enough alone,' she sighed.

But surely he'd get hurt, I thought. Seeing him there, in the circle of large, angry people, he looked more shaky and undersized than ever.

'Em – shouldn't we call him back? I mean . . .'

Em gazed at me levelly.

'People have a great deal of respect for Michael,' she said calmly. 'You'd be surprised. Besides, he's not as wobbly as he's making out. Cunning, he is.'

I stared at him again. True – come to think of it, Michael hadn't been using his stick much lately. Yet now he was leaning on it for all he was worth, looking pretty frail. Perhaps Em was right. There were plenty of big, strong, angry men in there already, and it certainly wasn't making anything any better. Still, I worried about him. I walked up and stood beside my dad, right behind Michael. My eyes met Jim's, opposite, and he gave a slight nod. A heat seemed to come off the crowd, once you were in the middle of it. There was the smell of sweat, the scraping of boots, the little bickers as bodies jostled.

Michael was talking, his voice weak compared to everyone else's; this had the effect of making everyone 'Shhh' each other and be quiet so that they could hear.

'Mr Simpson's right,' said Michael. 'We've all paid for this ambulance, and any one of us might need it at any moment. It could be *you, your* child, *your* mother . . .' As he spoke, he pointed to different people in the crowd around him.

'And what do you look like? Have you thought about that? We are villagers. People from the big towns think we're second class. Well, are we? Do we look civilised, today? If this was on the television news?'

People muttered, looked at their feet.

'*Villagers Destroy Own Ambulance.* And – and what would be next? What were you planning? To hang the driver and his family from the nearest tree?' Louder murmurs of protest greeted this. Michael went on. 'Well – what then? Someone was going to get hurt at the very least, weren't they? That tends to happen when people smash windscreens and drag people out. Or tip over the van they are in?'

The loud-voiced woman stepped forward and pushed back her dark, curly hair.

'Listen, we were angry. We were just trying to stop them, make a point. They've got a fuel-cell vehicle for ambulance use only, from the government. They were using it for a day out, a picnic, for God's sake! Like in the old days. Them and us. They had no right. Everyone had suspected it for ages, then we caught them, red-handed. None of us meant them to come to harm. Just the men got a bit overexcited.'

People nodded. The man who had grabbed the pickaxe looked shocked. 'I might have been going to smash the door open, but all the rest of you were trying to tip the thing over,' he growled. 'Don't try and paint it any other way.'

Dad held up his hand.

'Let's not talk about who's to blame. The police will be here in a minute. How about if we tell the driver to take the ambulance back and we all clear off, for now?'

The mention of police seemed to do the trick. People nodded and started to move away. Dad went over to the ambulance. The driver, sensing it was safe enough, opened his window to talk.

'Take it back home, get your family back in the house, lock the doors,' was all Dad said. He took no notice of the man's thanks, as if he hadn't heard. As the ambulance slowly did a U-turn, a few people jeered, and someone thumped at the back doors as it drove off, but the real anger seemed to have melted away.

Michael was talking to Brian Simpson.

'Do they still have those village council meetings at the hall?' he asked.

'Yes,' said Simpson. 'I'm a councillor, actually.'

'Everyone should talk about this. Otherwise it'll brew up again,' said Michael.

Simpson nodded and clapped his hands loudly so that people stopped in their tracks.

'Extraordinary General Meeting at the village hall tomorrow night. Seven p.m. We'll discuss this then,' he called, adding, as people nodded and walked away, 'Like proper, civilised people.'

Just as I was still reeling over Michael's surprising role in all this, Jim Simpson came up suddenly and grabbed my hand and shook it.

'What . . . I mean . . . why?' I stammered, staring at him.

'Tell your mum thanks, from me,' said Jim.

'My *mum?*' I called after him, puzzled. 'Jim! Wait!'

But he'd gone.

12

Van's Secret

<u>April 26th</u>

I'm writing this as the wind is picking up. It has a dark, dangerous sound to it, in keeping with the mood that seems to be hanging over us lately. After our little skirmish in the village the other day, which settled down after a meeting at the village hall, me and Em watched the news. More wars, while experts kept repeating that the root of them was down to overcrowding and not enough resources to go round — except there would be, if people would just learn to share. No one seems to be listening. The only things interrupting the fighting are more flooding, landslides, drought, disease, massive bush fires, and so-called 'silent' earthquakes, triggered by huge rainfalls. We watched the aerial footage, as we do every night. Little humans struggling to help. Not enough money.

But somehow there is always the money for guns and bombs.

On the home news, two celebrities were killed when angry activists found they had a private jet they were using. Seems they'd tried to sabotage it to stop it taking off, but only succeeded in causing it to crash after take-off. An anonymous message from the attackers offered a sort-of apology.

We are used to all this, of course, but tonight I feel tired of it all. It seems such a struggle. Things were easier, once. People used to have heating on, all day, when it was cold, even if they weren't in the house. They drove about alone, in cars which would seat five, for very little reason other than they felt like it. They bought things they didn't need — electrical gizmos and gadgets, just for amusement. We hate them, or laugh at them, looking back; but sometimes, just sometimes, I have a tinge of envy. Like last night, when we had used up our hour of television, so we switched it off, and hurried to bed before it got too dark and chilly to sit up any longer.

Then this morning, there was the post and a bit of good news, in that our application for Van's permit had been received and someone would come and inspect the 'working' horse, but not for another few days. This would give Jack a bit more time.

He's been doing well, following the book, which he's taken home to study. He struggles to read it, but seems better since I told him to go ahead and put his finger under each word if that helps. It does help, but he explained he was embarrassed to be seen following the print like that.

'What's worse?' I said. 'Someone seeing you do that when you read, or you not reading at all? Everyone does that when they're learning to read – like stabilisers on a bike. Keep your stabilisers until you don't need them any more.'

I helped yesterday because Jack's dad was busy doing the storm shutters on both our houses. I led Van while Jack walked behind him, holding our rope reins. Finally, I let go and although the horse faltered and stopped a couple of times with no one alongside him, eventually he obeyed Jack's clicking and flapping at the ropes and walked in front of him. They looked like a plough horse and his driver without a plough, but we all watched, quite proud, as Jack stopped, started and turned Van carefully around the meadow. Then he went out and around the lanes, with me walking behind – yes, me! – just in case Van needed leading again. It was one of those glorious but strange days, with the sky a dark, threatening blue, but with sudden flashes as the sun burst out and made the trees and grass and everything green, glow and shimmer, and the seagulls glinted like white metal as they soared.

I didn't get left behind, and people stopped what they were doing to look up when they heard Van's hooves ringing out, and quite a few came to talk to me when they recognised me, including my old school friend Tom, who seemed quite impressed and promised to come round.

But this afternoon, everything changed. Maybe we should have left things there, as Van had done so well, but instead we decided to sort the harness out once and for all, and learn to put it on. Only with the harness could Van actually pull something.

We laid out the harness on the floor, looked at the pictures in the book, and soon realised where everything was supposed to go – it wasn't as complicated as it looked, when you did that. There was a bridle for the head, with a metal bit which went in the horse's mouth, a collar which went around his neck, so he could lean on it and pull with his shoulders, and straps which went along the sides and crossed the horse's rump. If you wanted to pull something like a cart, you just put the shafts of the cart into holders which attached to the side straps.

Van stood patiently while I found the pages in the book and Jack got ready to put on the harness.

'Right,' said Jack – holding the collar and the rest of the harness in one hand, and the bridle in the other – 'What does the book say?'

'It says put the collar over the horse's head,' I read.

'OK,' said Jack. 'Here goes.' He put down the bridle and slipped the heavy, padded collar over Van's nose, and up over his ears, then down over his neck until it rested on his shoulders. The strapping for the horse's body then hung down around Van in a tangle. He stood there like an old professional, almost dozing as the sunlight flitted across his back from behind the blue-grey clouds.

Then we realised we should have put the bridle on first.

Jack pulled off the headcollar and either by luck, kindness, or because he didn't know he was free, Van stood motionless. Then Jack slipped the bridle half over Van's head and the metal bit bounced then pressed against Van's muzzle. He flung his head up, irritated. Jack tried again and the same thing happened. When Van's head went up, Jack had to strain on tiptoe.

'He's not opening his mouth for the bit to go in,' he said at last, exasperated.

'I was a bit worried about that,' I said, 'the way the book just says, "Put on the bridle", and "Get the bit in his mouth". How? I wish Simon was here.'

Jack tried again, managing to hold the bit in his other hand, and this time he got Van's lips apart, but the bit merely pressed against a very big set of clenched teeth. Van shook Jack off as if he were a fly, and put his head down to graze. I felt slightly panicky — the horse was now without any rope or reins and could run off if he felt like it, with the rest of the harness on.

We heard a quiet footfall, and there was Em, watching with her arms folded.

'Can't get the bit in,' explained Jack. He looked hot and flustered and one of his thumbs was starting to bleed where a buckle must have caught the skin around the nail.

'I don't blame him,' said Em. 'I wouldn't want that great hunk of metal in my mouth. I wonder how they are ever persuaded. I'm trying to remember what my friend did with her horse, but I don't think I ever watched. Hmm.' And she stood, looking thoughtful.

At that moment, Jack's mum peered over the fence. 'Why are you all standing watching him eat?' she called cheerfully. Jack explained. 'Oh,' she said. 'That's a shame. He sticks just about anything else in his mouth, doesn't he? Greedy thing. I caught him leaning over the fence and pulling the new leaves off our fruit trees this morning.'

'That's it!' said Em, smiling at Jack's mum. 'Like children with medicine. Let's make it taste good. Let me think.' Then: 'Sugar!' they both said together, and laughed.

'But sugar's expensive!' Jack frowned, but Em had already turned down his mum's offer of a little and was heading towards the kitchen.

After a few minutes, she reappeared with a small pudding basin and a spoon.

'The oven was still hot from baking the bread, so I managed to make the sugar into a syrup. Take the spoon, Jack, that's it, and slop some on the bit.' We watched as Jack wiped the gloopy mixture over the metal. The chinking sound of the spoon in the bowl made Van look up from his grazing and prick his ears. He pushed out his big, furry nose to investigate.

'I think he can smell it!' called Jack's mum encouragingly.

Jack slipped the noseband over Van's muzzle, and once again pressed the bit to the horse's lips. Van put back his ears a little and started to raise his head out of reach then suddenly paused, flicked his ears forward again, fumbling the bit with his lips and starting to rasp at the sticky metal with his long tongue.

'Quick!' squealed Em. 'Put it in his mouth before he licks it all off!'

Jack, who had seemed a bit surprised by Van's reaction, realised she was right and seized the moment, slipping the bit over the horse's tongue and getting the rest of the bridle on as fast as he could.

'There!' he said. 'He can't get it off now. Eugh!' And he wiped his hands on his jeans.

Van stood champing his bit like a kid with a lollipop while I gathered up the metres of reins so he couldn't tread in them.

We all rubbed Van's nose and patted his neck to tell him he'd done well.

'He doesn't seem to mind it, does he?' asked Jack, relieved. 'I'll lead him around in it first to check it's all right, and then I'll try walking behind him like before.'

He gathered up the reins from me and held them in a coil. Then he gave a little pull at the noseband with his other hand and the two of them were off, walking gently around the field, Jack alongside Van's head, gradually trying the reins to stop, start and turn, and finding they worked very well.

'You can tell he's done this before,' he called as he came back towards us. 'He's fine with it, isn't he?'

He reached the fence. 'Hold his head for a moment, would you Michael, while I take the reins behind him. We'll do a circuit like that.'

Jack's mum, having seen all was well, smiled and turned to go back to her vegetables. I held the reins under Van's chin as Jack went round behind him. I didn't really see what happened next. All I knew was that the reins were suddenly ripped from my fingers and something like a speeding train smashed my arm and shoulder out of the way and the next minute, I was on the ground. I heard Em and Jack's mum shouting and then Jack: 'Van! NO!'

I managed to roll on to my back and there, silhouetted against the glowering sky, was a huge, wild horse, rearing high, ears flattened back to his skull, nostrils flared blood-red, lips curled back. Then he plunged down with a thud which shook the earth and sent dust flying into the air, before leaping forwards with a tremendous surge of muscle and sinew, lashing out wildly with his back legs.

'Let go, Jack! Let go!' screamed Em and Jack's mum together. I gasped. I could just about make out the shape of Jack in the dust, somewhere on the ground behind the furious flailing hooves.

Then the horse was away, galloping across the field, bucking and squealing, and I felt Em's hands on my shoulders, grabbing so tight it hurt, shouting, 'Michael! Are you all right?'

'Yes,' I said, though my arm and fingers throbbed. 'What about Jack?'

Jack's mum was over the fence in a flash – I don't know how – and I stared from the ground as the dust settled, terrified of what I might see. If those hooves had hit Jack's head . . . they would have been like two sledgehammers, powered by a mighty engine. He just wouldn't *have* a head any more.

'Don't fuss, Mum! I'm fine. Michael! Are you all right?'

It was Jack's voice, and, if he could speak, I supposed he still had a head. The dust cleared and we found ourselves sitting and staring at each other. Jack's face was a mask of grime and his hair, ruffled crazily, was covered in the same greyish dust. The whites of his eyes shone out, startled. He looked as if he was in one of those school plays pretending to be an old man, with talc on his hair and face. I started to laugh. When Jack realised I wasn't having some sort of fit, he started to laugh too.

'You should see your face!' he giggled, staggering to his feet.

Em grabbed me and Jack's mum grabbed him, as if to check we were truly in one piece. They seemed to get grumpier the more we laughed, until Jack asked them if they'd be happier if we'd been badly injured and groaning.

But then we looked across at Van, standing under the hedge at the far end of the field, flinching and shivering, and we realised the seriousness of what had happened.

'I'd better go and catch him, and take the harness off,' said Jack, sounding defeated. We watched as he walked across the field, head down, shoulders hunched. When he came up beside Van, the horse jumped, startled, and looked as if he were about to bolt away.

'Oh, dear,' said Jack's mum. 'I hope he hasn't lost his trust, now.'

But we saw Jack stand still and call to Van, and the horse turned his head, put his ears forward, and walked towards him. Carefully, Jack took up the trailing reins and led him back to us.

'I can't think what set him off like that,' said Em, as they arrived at the fence.

'Neither can I,' said Jack. 'You'd think it might be the bit, as we haven't used one before, but I led him in it and pulled on it to stop and steer and it didn't bother him at all.'

'It seemed to be when you went behind him,' said his mum.

'No "seemed to be" about it. That's when it happened. But I've been walking behind him for a few days now. Never bothered him before.' Jack carefully undid buckles and slid the collar and harness off, then, finally, the bridle. Van turned away and began to graze.

'How strange,' I said. 'It's just like nothing ever happened. At least, it doesn't look like he holds a grudge. Doesn't seem frightened of us.'

'He was a bit odd when I approached to catch him,' said Jack, 'but he'd just been scared, so I suppose that's fair enough.'

But scared of what?

13

A Blinding Flash

While Michael was writing his diary in the early evening of that disastrous day, next door I was gloomily clearing the plates from our meal.

Rain was starting to smatter against the storm shutters, driven by a gusty wind. Dad was winding up the radio, though it was wound enough by now, and we'd already heard the storm warning.

'You can't expect it all to go smoothly,' he said, noticing my silence. 'There are bound to be setbacks. Especially with this horse. We knew there was a problem. Otherwise, you'd never have got him.'

'I know. I just don't like it that I don't know what we did wrong,' I said, putting the plates in the washing-up bowl.

'You didn't do anything wrong, necessarily. Well, not according to the book. Maybe you did according to Van.' He smiled, came over and ruffled my hair. 'Ugh! You're all gritty! There's enough electric for a warm shower, anyway. At least with this wind the turbine will be working hard. If it doesn't get ripped off, of course.'

We paused and listened to the deep, steady whine of the wind. With the storm shutters closed, you couldn't see out, that was the trouble. What was coming? How close was it?

I thumped at the foot pedal under the sink to pump water into the bowl. Like Dad, I needed something to do while we waited for the storm. It was getting noisier outside, but here inside, with the house feeling wrapped and bolted down, there was an eerie silence, broken only by the annoying squeak and thump of the foot pedal.

'Where's Mum?' I asked suddenly.

'Final locking up and general flapping around the blasted hens,' said Dad irritably. 'Good point. I'll go out and get her in.'

Before he could reach it, the back door opened, and Mum stood there, accompanied by a freezing draught.

'James! It's Van – he's very scared. I think he might jump out of the field. Maybe we should put him in one of the outhouses or something,' she said urgently.

I rushed to the door and looked out. The sky was growing dark for this early in the evening, and huge, sludge-coloured clouds were flying across it. I strained to see over the fence, shivering in the cold without my coat. I couldn't see Van at first, but then I saw a shape moving near the distant hedge and realised it was the horse, mane and tail flying. The wind made the grass ripple in silver sheets, which turned to green, then silver again, like a strange ocean; Van galloped across it, his beauty taking my breath away. He scooted to a stop near Michael's garden fence, snorted and rolled his eyes, then swung away and cantered back up the field, following the fence as if seeking a way out.

'Get back in the house,' Dad ordered, running past me. Mum stood in the doorway, watching worriedly.

'You'll need the headcollar,' I called, and

snatching it up from the nail by the back door, I ran after him. I doubted Dad would catch him. I wasn't sure *I* would be able to. Van had changed again, from a placid friend to a wild horse. As I ran, the doubts I'd had after his crazy antics that afternoon began to surface and form themselves into one, clear fear. Was Van truly *unpredictable?* Was that the problem – that he would change in an instant from a calm creature, unbothered by barking dogs or flapping bags, to a wild animal, beautiful but deadly? Might he pull a cart one day, but the next rear, lash out, possibly bolt, for *no real reason at all*?

As I climbed the fence between our house and Michael's, I felt tears being dragged from my eyes by the wind. The trouble was, this wasn't just a business idea. If it all failed, Van could be shot and go in a freezer, nothing lost, nothing gained. No. A lot would be lost. I felt a wrenching in my chest. My heart. The horse was part of my heart now. I couldn't stand it. If he was too dangerous to keep, why couldn't he just run free, and be a wild thing? I knew the answer, of course. Because there wasn't room, there was no place left for such creatures.

Dad was ahead of me, already at the gate. He turned and waited impatiently for me.

'Van!' I called into the wind, with no real hope. He wouldn't hear me, and in any case, he was too frightened to listen.

But back at the top of the field, the glistening shape turned, ears pricked, and set off again at a canter, straight towards us, tail held up high like a flag.

'He's coming!' Dad yelled, above the roar of the wind.

In a moment, Van was there, snorting, pressing at the gate till I thought it might be pushed over. I fumbled with the headcollar.

'Steady, steady boy,' I said, slipping it over his nose. My fingers seemed to belong to someone else and I battled to do up the straps. Dad put his face close to mine so I could hear him above the noise of the wind.

'If he pulls a stunt like today, let him go, do you understand? You'll only be dragged if you hold on. If he wants to go, neither of us can stop him.

166

Promise?' And he gripped me by the shoulder.

'Promise,' I shouted back.

'Over there,' he pointed. 'Over there' was an old, tumbledown stone outhouse, with a big wooden door swinging in the breeze. I'd wandered through it with Michael a few times. It had nothing in it except some mouldy old timber propped against the far wall. We'd talked about turning it into a stable and somewhere to store the tack and cart.

I led Van towards it, with Dad walking the other side of him and holding on to the noseband, but he needn't have worried. Van seemed relieved we were with him and walked quickly but didn't play up.

We were almost there when quite suddenly, everything went incredibly dark. It was like we had suddenly been thrown into the middle of a pitch-black night.

'Get in, get in!' I heard Dad shout, and he started to run, dragging at Van's noseband. The horse broke into a trot and I ran beside him, and somehow all three of us got through the doorway at almost the same time, my shoulder smacking into the doorjamb on the way.

Inside, it was dark and smelled of woodland and mushrooms. Van spun around when we reached the back wall and dragged at the rope in my hands, heading for the doorway.

I braced my legs, dug my heels in the ground and pulled on the rope as hard as I could.

'No, Van. Whoa. Stand!'

Van stopped, snorted. I patted his neck and found it damp. A steady heat rose up from him and enveloped me.

'I'll get the door. Hang on to him,' said Dad, and rushed out to battle with it. To the side of me, though it was dark, I could see Van's large, brown eye staring into mine, full of worry, but still he stood, because I'd asked him to. I rubbed between his eyes and down his long nose, his favourite place.

'What a brave horse. What a good boy. You'll be all right now. Good boy,' I prattled. Dad almost had the door shut – he paused a moment, staring out.

'Oh, dear Lord. It's a tornado.'

Then, with a superhuman wrench, he dragged the door shut, and we were thrown into greater darkness, with just a little pool of light filtering down from gaps in the old roof.

Van jumped a little as Dad moved towards us, but he made the clucking sound he used to calm the chickens, and this seemed to work – Van pushed his nose out and sniffed at him in welcome.

We didn't say anything about getting back to the house. We both knew it was too late. We were going to have to see out the tornado here.

Rain started to pound on the roof in sudden flurries; it came through the gaps and hit the dust around us with little smacks and sizzles, releasing puffs of earthy scent. Van tensed all over – I laid my hand on his neck and felt the skin quivering. Dad, the other side of him, said softly: 'Hold on boy, all over soon.' I hoped so. I wondered whether it was safer to get close to the wall if the roof blew off, or whether it might fall on us. I wondered what Mum was thinking, now we'd got her in the house but we were out here.

Then came the most terrible demon drumming of hailstones – if the rain had been loud, this was like having your head in a tin bucket while someone hit it with hammers. I wanted to cover my ears, but Van started to shuffle and prance on the spot and nearly ripped the rope from my grasp, so I clung desperately to it with both hands. Then he swung away from me and I heard a muffled curse from Dad, so I knew he'd banged into him. I pulled as hard as I could on the rope and got the horse's head back towards me, but now his shoulder, hard as solid machinery, smacked into mine and sent me flying.

All the time, both me and Dad were shouting our calming words above the noise: 'Steady, steady, Van, good boy, it's just hail!' but I knew that shouting doesn't sound very calming to anyone.

I suddenly realised that me and Dad knew that the noise, terrible though it was, was just hail – but Van didn't. He couldn't see it. And then everything came to me in a blinding flash. That was it. He couldn't see it. The terror we all have, of lying in the dark and hearing some strange noise and not knowing what it is. If you get up and look and find it's just an old tree branch creaking outside, and a twig scraping the window, you can go back to sleep. I knew also that I'd just stumbled across something deeper, more important – but there wasn't time to think at that moment. Van reared right up and took the rope, with skin-shaving speed, from my hands. I looked up and saw him above me and to the side, lit like a fabulous unicorn in the ghostly light from the broken roof.

Then he crashed back down next to me, but was up on his hind legs again a fraction of a second later.

'Dad!' I shrieked. 'The door! Open the door!' But I couldn't tell if he'd heard me above the hammering sound of a million iron bolts being fired at the roof and walls. Van let out a tremendous, screaming neigh, full of rage and fear, and put his head down and started to fire out with his back legs, almost as if he were trying to kick down the stone walls. I heard Dad shout something, then Van charged towards the door, plunged to a stop and reared again in front of it, just missing hitting his head on the roof.

I ran, dodging the flailing front hooves, and grabbed hold of the handle of the door. Pointlessly, I shouted, 'Wait, Van, wait!' but he did back away as I fought to open it. Then, wonderfully, Dad's hands were on the handle with mine, and we both pushed, and the door flew back; Dad almost rugby-tackled me into the nearest corner, out of Van's way.

But Van stood, snorting, at the open door as the wind screamed into the building. There was a ripping sound as it punched its way through the roof, where there had been small gaps; now there was a gaping hole, and almost half of the roof had gone.

I peered over Dad's shoulder, and felt him turn to look through the door too. The sound of the hail was blasted away by a noise like masses of jet engines. Now the old stones and mortar, the very ground around us, shook and hummed, as if electricity coursed through it. I saw a column of what I thought was smoke. It was the tornado – like an explosion which was caught in a time loop, for ever in action, it swirled across the field. As it got closer, you could see bits and pieces whirling up and around, ever higher, until it hurt your neck to try and see the top of it. We cowered and watched – me, Dad and Van. Now it was only metres away, it seemed; we saw the nose of it, snaking, scenting. Don't find us, I thought, please don't; but I knew it was not a creature which could think, nor did it have the power to show mercy. Then suddenly, like Van at the open door, it stopped, swirled for seconds as if undecided, and shot away, away across the hedge and the trees beyond, running a half-circle around us and the two cottages.

Dad let me go and we straightened up. Van stood quietly; but listening, watching.

'He didn't run,' said Dad wonderingly. 'He was terrified, he wanted out, we opened the door, but he didn't run. I thought he was going to be past us or over us at full gallop as soon as we had the thing open.'

'It's because he could see what was out there, when we opened the door,' I said.

'Ah!' said Dad. 'Yes, that's a good point. Didn't fancy taking his chances in the tornado after all.'

'He was only frightened of the noise when he couldn't see what was making it.' I added, 'And I know that means . . . something important. But I can't quite get it straight yet. I think it has something to do with what went wrong today.'

'You mean, he sensed a tornado coming and got worked up? Animals can tell things like that, I suppose,' said Dad, reaching out and gently patting Van's neck.

'No, no. Not that. I'll think it over.' I wished I could put my finger on it, but my head was spinning with the noise and the shock of the past few minutes.

'Let's take the headcollar off, leave him here, and get back in the house quick,' said Dad. 'You never know, it might come back. Then Van can stay in or go out as he chooses.'

I stroked Van's nose, reluctant to leave him. Dad tugged my arm, gently but firmly. So I took off the headcollar and we headed out to the gate, and Van stayed where he was, watching us.

With the tornado's passing, the wind died, along with the hail and rain. It was suddenly strangely calm and quiet. The sky, though it was evening, had lightened a little. We went round Michael's house in the proper way – by the side path, instead of climbing the fence to our house – and then back up our drive. Dad surveyed the cottages as we walked; he didn't say anything, but I knew that he was relieved that the shutters and roofs had held together.

Mum jumped to her feet as we came through the kitchen door, flung her arms around us in turn, and listened as we told her what had happened. She shuddered. 'That animal could have killed several people today, with his great crashing hooves,' she said, but before I could rush to Van's defence, she added, 'but he didn't. And it must take some doing, if you are an animal that size, to miss everyone around you – especially when you're out of your mind with terror. I think he not only doesn't mean to hurt anyone, he's trying his best not to. That's something in his favour.'

The power grid was down, but our generator was fine, so we had enough for hot drinks and warm scones from the oven, and a light for the evening in one room at a time. We sat around talking, eating and drinking, tired, and we stayed up a little later than usual, but after the storm we needed time to wind down.

'I hope the rest of the village is OK,' said Mum. 'I suppose we'll go out tomorrow morning and see.'

'These old houses, they really are solid,' said Dad. 'They knew how to build them back then, though maybe they didn't expect such winds, so often. There will be a bit of flooding, but only at the dip in the main street, up to the bottom of some folks' doors, I reckon. Simpson will have had a fair bit, down there below us, but he's used to that.'

'That reminds me, Mum,' I said. 'Why did Jim Simpson ask me to thank you?'

Mum looked coy and shrugged.

Dad looked at her and chuckled.

'You were on to old Simpson about the boys,

weren't you, Val? What did you tell him, give them a bit of motherly love? I just can't see him tucking them up in bed at night with a kiss.'

When he said that, while realising it was an unlikely picture, I suddenly found it wasn't that funny. Because these were the sorts of things your mum did that I took for granted. And while old Brian Simpson wouldn't be doing it, that meant Fred and Jim never got those little bits of fuss any more. No one to cluck over a scratched knee and find a plaster, no one to check shoes still fitted or that there were clean socks. Much as I hadn't really liked the boys, I did feel a bit sorry for them.

'I just can't bear hearing people talk about their children as if they're useless, and in front of them,' Mum said, picking up our plates. 'And then they complain that the kids are no good. I know it's none of my business, but seeing as there was some fallout which affected our son, I decided to stick my nose in.' She clattered the plates in the sink.

'What did you say?' I asked.

'I just said they would become what he said they were. So perhaps he ought to keep noticing the things they did well instead of what they did badly, and tell them he'd noticed, too.'

'Ouch,' said Dad, still amused. 'And what did he say to that?'

Mum turned and faced him, folded her arms and looked stern.

'Actually, he was quite surprised. And very nice. I think for one thing, he liked to hear someone saying something supportive about his boys, instead of complaining about them. I think he liked someone coming up with helpful suggestions. He's not an expert at bringing up children without his wife – he's just trying to do the best he can, learning as he goes along. So he said he was going to try and do what I said.'

'Oh!' said my dad, looking impressed.

'Yes!' said my mum triumphantly.

'I think you mean yah boo sucks to you,' I offered helpfully as I stretched and yawned. 'I'm off to bed. I'll do those plates in the morning, Dad, if you leave them.'

That night, as I drifted off to sleep, my thoughts spun like the tornado, remembering how I'd realised that Van was frightened of things he could hear but not see, and how I'd known this was really important – but I couldn't work out why.

Then I was dreaming, and we were all there, as we had been that afternoon, putting on the harness by Michael's fence. But I could see myself, Jack, picking up the bridle, and suddenly I realised that I was seeing things from Van's point of view – I *was* Van. I felt the irritation as Jack tried to push a bit in my mouth – but then felt the sweet sensation of melting sugar as he tried again, and everything was fine. I trusted Jack, liked him next to me. Now I didn't quite understand what was happening in the dream. Something was wrong with my eyes – I seemed to be half blind. Everything was dark around, but I could see, as if in a tunnel, straight ahead. This was unsettling, but I heard Jack walking next to me, leading me, sometimes a little ahead so I could see his shoulder and the side of his head, and I could see where I was going, so it didn't seem too bad.

We walked back towards the fence; I could see Michael, and Em, and my – or should I say, Jack's

– mum. Michael put out his hand and held the reins – that was all right, I liked Michael – but suddenly I couldn't see him any more and I couldn't see Jack any more, and something was behind me; I heard a twig snap, and then it got close, and I thought it would pounce. I could almost feel the claws digging in my flanks, the teeth sinking in my back. I remembered a time this had happened before, the strange black darkness to the side and behind me, and I remembered the pain as I'd kicked out in terror into something hard behind me, heard shouts, felt a whip burning my back and a wrenching of the metal bit till it cut the sides of my mouth. Desperately, I turned my head and looked for Jack, beside me or behind me, where he always was, but I saw nothing, nothing but a terrible black darkness I couldn't understand.

The fear surged in my chest so strongly that I thought my heart would explode, and I woke, sweating, and found myself sitting up with the bedcovers thrown off. I gasped to get my breath back, trying to make sense of the dream. I had been Van, I'd felt what it had been like for him – what was the terrifying blackness, the blindness which had come over him? For a moment, I dreaded that there must be something wrong with his eyes – then I caught a glimpse of a moment in the dream again, like a still from a movie. Me, Jack, with the bridle in my hand. It had blinkers on it. That's what was different to everything we'd tried before. That was the cause of Van's terror. The blinkers.

14

After the Tornado

<u>April 24th</u>

Me and Em were slow and tired because the wind kept
us awake last night. Though we are used to such
things, it still has a way of making you wait till it's over
before you can really get to sleep.

I stopped on the landing to look out of the window,
as I always did, to check on Van. This morning, after the
terrible winds, I was relieved to see him grazing calmly,
as usual, picking his way around the bits of branch and
debris. Jack's dad was already out there, close behind
the horse with his wheelbarrow, collecting manure.

Just as we were eating breakfast, someone knocked
at the front door. It turned out to be Jack, bright and
early. This was unusual for him. We'd usually meet at
our gate when Simon came, or else I'd find Jack out in
the field, messing around with Van.

'Everything all right, Jack?' I asked him as I opened the door, sounding a bit muffled through the toast I was trying to swallow. 'Did your place survive the wind?'

'What? Oh, yes, thanks. It was a proper tornado, you know, we saw it from your outhouse. But the thing is—'

'Our outhouse? We? What were you doing?'

'Me and Dad. Mum thought he'd be better inside, because he was running about like a loony. Van, I mean, not Dad. But he wasn't.'

'He wasn't what? You mean your mum made it up about him running around like a loony?'

'No, no, he was – I mean, he wasn't better inside. But it's all right because—'

Em interrupted from behind me in the hallway.

'Any particular reason Jack can't come in and you two can't continue this fascinating discussion over breakfast?' she said sarcastically. 'Only you said you were going to pour the tea, Michael, and it'll be cold soon.'

We went in and sat down, which was probably for the best as Jack calmed down and we made him start with the story of the tornado and Van's outburst in the outhouse, so that we could follow what he was talking about.

'So then, after the dream, I realised what my brain had already worked out,' he finished triumphantly. 'That Van is frightened of things he can't see, at the least, and is probably extra frightened when he can't see and doesn't understand why he's suddenly blind, on top of that.'

'Hmmm,' said Em, which is a habit of hers when she's thinking carefully.

'Well, so what's your plan?' I asked. 'Try again without the blinkers, I suppose?' I stirred my tea and pushed Jack's cup closer to him to remind him to drink it.

'I suppose,' said Jack, a little less certainly. 'Though I thought we'd ask Simon this morning. I don't remember seeing any horse pulling a cart or even a plough without blinkers. So there must be a good reason for them.'

We thought about it too, and admitted we hadn't seen such a thing either.

'Here,' said Jack, pushing one of my old diaries towards me, 'I almost forgot. I brought this back for you.'

'What's that?' asked Em. 'One of Michael's? You poor thing! If you want something to read I've got plenty of good books.'

'He's not really reading it, Em,' I said, swatting at her with it. 'He was just practising his writing, weren't you Jack?' I pulled out a loose sheet from between the pages and saw lines of neat, slightly familiar writing on it. 'Look, here's some — did you do this, Jack?'

He nodded.

'It's not quite the same, but it does look good, doesn't it? I mean, you can read it, not like before.' He looked from me to Em, anxiously.

Em peered over my shoulder.

'It's good that it's not quite the same. You want it to be your own style. Yes, I can read it fine. Looks very neat. Not that I've seen your writing before, so I don't know how much of an improvement this is.'

'A *big* improvement,' said Jack feelingly. 'But it didn't take that long to get the hang of it. I started by trying and throwing away anything I didn't like, and that was good, because I knew no one was going to see it. Then I stopped chucking it away and saved this bit, because it didn't look bad at all. I don't know why they don't teach you to write like that in school.'

'Well, different things suit different people, I expect,' I said. 'Some kids might find it a bit boring doing it this way, who knows. I think maybe they taught it like that hundreds of years ago, when they did lots of things wrong, so it probably got chucked out as too old-fashioned. Anyway, give us your cup, Jack and I'll rinse it up. We want to be ready for Simon, so we can ask about the blinkers.'

When Simon arrived, we were waiting at the gate. Jack just about managed to contain himself while Simon told us what a difficult journey he'd had, trying to get round fallen trees and stopping all the time to lift debris out of his path from the winds last night. Then Jack told Simon what had happened when we'd tried the full harness, and his face clouded as he listened. Next Jack explained what had happened in the barn, and Simon's frown became deeper and he shook his head.

'But I think it's all right,' added Jack excitedly, seeing Simon's expression. 'It was the blinkers which made him go mad. He was frightened because he couldn't see what was behind him.'

Simon looked puzzled.

'Did he have blinkers on in the barn, then?' he asked.

'No, no. But it was the same thing. He couldn't see

anything. Once we opened the door, he saw the tornado, the hail and everything. Then he calmed down and stayed where he was. But my question is, why do they wear blinkers when they pull things? Can we just leave them off?'

Simon looked unconvinced. Thank goodness Jack hadn't mentioned the dream, I thought.

'I think you'll find he just went mad because he doesn't fancy working, I'm afraid,' he said, sighing. 'He's done it before and he'll do it again. The danger in a horse like that is you never know when, so he's worse than useless. It's no good if he's all right some of the time – that's like a dog that generally won't attack and bite, but might occasionally. He might just as well do it all of the time, because it means you can never trust him. I think it's just a coincidence that it happened when you put the blinkers on. And the barn – that was simple claustrophobia – the fear of being trapped in a small space. Lots of horses won't have the top stable door done up, whatever the weather or noise. A few won't tolerate any stable at first, or won't be left in one alone. When you opened the door, he just didn't feel trapped any more. He saw the weather and decided to stay put, but mostly because he felt he was free to run if he wanted.'

Jack's face fell. He was surprised and disappointed at Simon's reaction, I knew. He was aware, too, that me and Em were listening and was worried that he now sounded like a fool next to Simon, who knew more.

'What about not using the blinkers, just in case we want to try it?' I asked, to back him up a little. 'What are they for, anyway?'

'The idea is, they're to stop a working horse shying at things to the side of him, which would be very dangerous with machinery or a cart or carriage full of people attached—' said Simon.

Jack interrupted.

'But Van proved he doesn't do that when we went around the lanes.'

'That's as may be,' continued Simon, 'but the other reason for blinkers is that the horse never really understands something is attached to him, and it's believed if he saw it moving behind him when he moved, he'd bolt.'

'Goodness!' said Em. 'Have you ever tried Spud without?'

'No,' chuckled Simon, eyeing the rump of the horse in front of him. 'And I'm not about to, either.' Spud, perhaps hearing his name, shifted a step forward and the wheels on the cart creaked.

'Seems a bit risky,' I said. 'All of this based on a trick. What if the blinkers ever came off?'

'Never heard of that happening,' said Simon. 'And the system seems to have worked for centuries without a problem. So, in answer to your question,' here he looked sternly at Jack, 'it sounds like the horse has proved himself dangerous enough already, and I couldn't advise you to risk yourselves – and others,' he shot a look at me and Em, '– any further.'

'Oh,' said Jack, and looked down at the ground. 'Oh. All right then, Simon.'

'Thanks, Simon, for all your advice,' Em remembered to say.

'Sorry, lad,' called Simon, seeing Jack turn away, head down, making for his house. 'You gave it a darn good try, anyway. Not your fault.'

'Don't worry, Simon, I'll talk to him. And thanks again,' I said quietly, and then he and Spud were off and away down the lane. I stood and watched them go.

'Amazing,' I said to Em. 'There goes Spud, clip clop; Simon is up high behind him in the seat going click click with his tongue; and the wheels and the timber go creak, creak. And yet Spud doesn't know it's following him, tied on to him. Though he passes other horses with carts every day. And he doesn't find them frightening, either. I'd never taken horses to be so stupid – though I didn't know much about them before, I'll admit.'

'No,' said Em slowly, 'neither had I. Both of my friends' horses were pretty clever, it seemed to me. Do you know, the big horse had a game where he took the brushes from behind her back while she was grooming him? Every time she changed brushes, he'd snatch the one she'd put down without her seeing, and put it over the other side of himself. She kept stopping and looking for them and thought she was going potty. And the pony had a party trick. He'd worked for a carter before she'd had him, and they must have visited the pubs. He could take the top off a beer bottle with his lips and drink out of it – they knew because he did it with one of her dad's one day, when he'd put it down for a moment. You had to be careful not to put any type of bottle within his reach.'

We looked at each other, thinking.

'What's the worst that can happen,' she said, smiling, 'if we take care?'

I remember this all so vividly.

I don't know why, but I'd expected Simon to go along with my idea, I suppose. I never thought he would react in the way he did, so when he said Van was dangerous – like a dog that randomly attacked, and we all know what happens to them – I was really shocked. I felt angry for Van; scared that Simon, the expert I relied upon, was telling me to give up. It felt like I had just been cast adrift, not knowing where I was, in the middle of a huge and terrifying ocean. And Michael and Em – they would put my safety first. They wouldn't want my parents to be cross with them for helping me do something dangerous. And in all honesty, I couldn't risk *their* safety with my crazy idea, which an expert had just rubbished. To my horror, my throat closed up and tears started to well behind my eyes. So I had to turn and walked away.

I realised vaguely that Michael and Em were

talking by the gate in low tones as I did so, and I thought they were probably saying how sad and terrible the whole business was. Maybe they were even working out the practical details, like wondering who should call Brian Simpson with his gun and knives to get Van out of the way as soon as possible; I didn't know or care. I slammed up the path and into our house, up the stairs, to my bedroom.

I hadn't been there long when I heard a tap at the front door, and then Dad's feet along the hall as he went to answer it. I thought it was probably Michael, but no one called me. I blew my nose and went into the bathroom to wash my face. Then I went and sat back on my bed again to wait for the fury of feelings in my chest to die down.

I liked my bedroom. I couldn't seem to think, so I just sat there and gazed around. Seeing the familiar things around me was kind of comforting. Creamy, cracked paint, bulging walls, low beams, the little window which looked over the lane. My shelves full of old tools and dusty pens, the odd sock, a seashell which had another tiny shell inside it which you couldn't get out, and a stone which might be an ancient flint arrowhead – or just a bit of flint which happened to be that shape. Then there were photos of Gran, others of me, Mum and Dad in the *Aunt May*, stuck on the wall without frames and starting to curl at the corners. My eyes wandered to my desk, with another of Michael's diaries on it, and my attempts at writing spread all over the place – the screwed-up versions, like hard, cracked snowballs, clustered on the floor beneath.

I cheered up a bit seeing that. A funny little idea, a fair bit of time and effort which I hadn't really noticed, and it had worked. I got up and went and looked at the latest thing I'd written. This time, I hadn't copied from Michael. I'd written a bit about Van, because I didn't know what else to write about. The writing was neat and I knew that, strangely enough, my spelling was pretty good too. This had happened without really trying. Because Michael's spelling was good, I'd got used to reading and copying particular words. When I wrote them by myself now, I either remembered how they were spelled because of the copying or, if I did start to spell something wrong, I could just see it looked wrong straight away. I supposed it was a little like the way you expect a dog to have four legs, and a bird to have two and wings. You just got used to seeing them like that. You didn't have to memorise it or anything to know.

'It frightens Van to be suddenly blind,' I read, following the words with my finger across the rough paper, 'and I don't blame him. All horses can't be the same, just like people aren't all the same. If he manages to do his work just fine without blinkers, then that's the way it will be.'

Like me, I thought suddenly. If I had to read and write by doing this – copying some writing I liked, and holding my finger under the word I was reading – then that's the way it had to be. It didn't matter how, so long as you did it. It was definitely better than not doing it at all, and failing. And I was lucky, in that no one was planning to chop me up and put me in the freezer if I refused to read or write.

'Jack!'

My dad's voice broke into my thoughts. I heard the front door close. Whoever had come to talk to him had gone. I went out to the landing and leaned over the banisters.

'What is it?'

Dad looked up at me. He had his coat on.

'Me and your mum feel we ought to go and see how the rest of the village got on with that tornado – just in case anyone needs some help. You coming?'

'Oh – yes, OK.' I'd thought he was going to talk about Van – especially if that had been Michael calling. I felt selfish and slightly guilty when I remembered that other people might have bigger problems of their own.

For so many reasons, I will never forget that day. Outside it was calm, bright, with not a breath of wind. Mum, Dad and me went out of our gate into the lane and as we walked along it was as if some kind of machine had worked the hedges and trees. Either side of us, glints of white gold shone out as the sun touched the bushes – I looked more closely and realised the white gold was bare, raw new timber – branches had been flayed, stripped of leaf and twig and bark, which now carpeted the lane we walked.

Dad faltered as we passed the entrance to the lane which led down to the Simpsons' place. 'I hope they're all right,' he said doubtfully. 'I suppose we must check the village first.'

'Yes,' said Mum, 'Brian did say they were used to the odd flood, anyway. We'll call on the way back.'

We carried on, and did not see or hear another person. It's true that you could walk this lane without bumping into anyone, but usually *someone* was about. The silence and stillness was eerie. We started to see larger and larger branches and boughs of trees which had crashed down. They had already been moved to the side of the road so that vehicles could pass. The closer we got to the centre of the village the bigger the branches, and Mum and Dad's faces became serious-looking. We passed cottages on either side with great sections of roof missing, where the tiles had been stripped in rows, like giant dominos snatched up by a monstrous vacuum cleaner. A mighty tree had fallen near one house, managing to miss it by centimetres. Further on, the glinting trees and bushes were decorated with clothing, shoes. On one side of us, heavy, twisted metal – who knew what it once belonged to? – was beaten and wrapped around a lamppost. Bundles of feathers, big and small, began to appear amongst the twigs and leaves at our feet. We stepped around them; the poor birds had been dashed from the trees. Dad stopped and gazed at a mangled piece of engine from a fuel-cell car. He kicked at a single tyre which had ended up next to it. 'Just look at it!' he said. 'And what happened to the rest of it?'

We walked on, more slowly, because we were reaching the high point in the lane which looked down on to the shops and everything in the centre of the village, and I think we were scared of what we were going to see.

Well, at least everything was still there. That was the first thing I thought as we gazed down on the chaos. A scummy brown lake had formed, about half a metre deep at its worst, in the dip where the village green had been. People waded slowly through it, their movements weary. Some of the buildings had their roofs peeled off as if with a giant can-opener, or large holes smashed in them. Over everything, it looked as if someone had emptied bag loads of rubbish.

One of the graceful, tall, brick buildings on our left had a massive spear of wood stuck into its shiny front door, and marks all over it as if it had been attacked with axes. It made you imagine hordes of knights in armour, and the days of bows and arrows. 'How could the wind do *that*?' I gasped.

'Tile strike,' said Dad, pointing. There were smashed clay tiles and slates on the ground around and one or two still sticking out of the woodwork, when I looked closely. 'Much of the damage and the danger is from what the wind picks up and hurls, more than the wind itself. It took the tiles from the other buildings, then fired them.'

Further on, there were other examples of the strange and cruel tricks the wind could play. A piano, with barely a scratch on it, neatly placed astride the high wall around the village hall, our school. 'How on earth will they get that down?'

wondered my dad. A child's big, brightly coloured plastic cartoon rocking horse grinned smugly from behind the black iron railings in front of one of the smart town houses. 'Oh!' said my mum. 'That's the Levys' house – everyone knows how unhappy they've been since they lost a baby and then found out they can't have any more children. Oh, how awful – we have to move it, James.' I had a feeling the poor Levy couple had probably seen it by now, but I stood back and watched as my parents grappled with the ridiculous creature and followed as they carried it out of sight of the house and put it down on the pavement.

The wind had spared the menders and the cart business next door, and only smashed a small pane of glass at the old ladies' general store, but there was a crowd around the Princes' clothes shop, and as we drew closer, starting to splash in the deepening water, we could see that all the windows were gone and a huge tree seemed to have toppled across it, taking out the roof and almost cutting the place in two. We waded in closer and saw old Josh and Harry Acre passing bolts of fabric over their heads to people waiting outside. 'Steady now!' voices called. 'Keep it dry and clean!' The sound of sawing came from somewhere.

Dad tapped a back nearest to us. The man turned. It was Brian Simpson.

'Brian. We were wondering if there was anything we could do?' asked Dad. 'Is your place all right? We were going to call in and check on the way back.'

'Not too bad, thanks,' he said. 'We put the flood boom all around last night, worked a treat. Nothing but a little leak or two. But we do need your help here. We thought we could manage, but I was just about to send Fred for you.' His face grew serious. 'We're getting out any stock we can save, but we don't know yet whether the Princes will be here to appreciate it. The tree has trapped them in the back, in their bedroom behind the shop, apparently. We can hear her, but not him. Go and see.'

He stepped out of the way and I felt the cold water oozing over my boots and soaking my trousers as we waded past the people passing material and clothes backwards in a line.

'You can get into the shop,' said Josh Acre, in his quiet way, from just inside the door. We waited for a moment, but he didn't add anything.

Harry wiped his filthy hands on his shirt, which was already the colour of the floodwater.

'This way. You can get as far as the back of the shop, but the tree has smashed right down in front of the entrance to their living quarters, so we can't get though,' he explained rapidly, and pointed behind him. I looked and I think my mouth hung open. I couldn't remember seeing a tree that wide around its middle before in my life. There seemed to be metres of huge, grey, elephant-skinned trunk, lying right along the wall behind him and stretching up through the ceiling. It looked like part of a giant prehistoric monster. 'So round the back door looks the most likely,' Harry rattled on at speed, 'but there's one hefty great bough across it and from what Mrs Prince says, another bit of that has crushed Mr Prince as he lay in bed. The men are sawing as fast as they can, but we don't have a chance of shifting it, even when it's free, in my opinion, however many strong men lend a hand. Their idea is to saw it into little bits if they have to – but I think that will take so long, it'll be too late for Mr Prince.'

'I reckon that's right,' added Josh quietly.

Poor Mr Prince, I thought, remembering the kind smile and the twinkling eyes, the way he spoke to a kid like me just the same as if I'd been a rich, grown-up man who'd been his customer for years and years. And Mrs Prince, with her gentle jokes and teasing, and the sweets for children hidden under the counter, which she passed you the minute you came in and again when you left. I wondered if the invisible wall of silence between them had been shattered with the bricks of the house. Was he crying out to her in pain? Was she telling him it was all right, help was on the way?

'We'll go round the back then,' said Mum, and she was off out of the door again like a shot, with me and Dad sloshing after her.

When we got around the back, we saw that the branch of the huge tree had crashed through the roof, and the shape of it meant that it also curved over the back door and pinned it shut. Several men were working big double saws, one to each end, and there were ropes tied to various parts of the branch, going off at angles. When they saw us they cheered as if the cavalry had arrived, which I thought was a bit strange, but I supposed it was because people had heard about Dad's talents.

'Oh, dear,' said Mum, then added, 'The windows – surely someone could get through the window?'

One of the men jumped down from where he was tying a rope. As he came towards us, I realised it wasn't really a man, it was Jim Simpson.

'Hello there!' he said, looking very pleased to see us. 'Someone *has* got through the window – Fred, as he was small enough. He talked to Mrs Prince – she probably could get through the window, at a push, but she won't without her husband. Mr Prince – well, Fred didn't say much, just went a bit green, so I don't think it's a pretty sight. Reckoned he was alive though, or at least, Mrs Prince told him he was – he didn't want to get close to check. Unconscious at the least, he said. Certainly we can't get him out through the window

– he'll have to come out on a board for the ambulance. And there's another problem.'

'Another?' asked Dad, wiping his forehead.

'Tree across the ambulance garage door, can you believe? Driver and his family been sawing at it as soon as they found out. Think they've some help now. But you could call by, with the horse, before you come back here. No good us getting him out and we can't get him to hospital.'

We all nodded, sympathetic and serious as we stood knee deep in filthy water, listening. Then we seemed to hear the last bit properly, a moment after he'd spoken.

'Sorry, the *horse*?' said Dad.

Jim looked surprised.

'But that's why you've come, isn't it? Dad was about to send Fred to ask . . . You've the only one in the village, everyone knows that. A few of us hoped the carrier might offer, but he turned off by the top lane as soon as he saw the flood, so no one could ask. Horse is all right, isn't he? He didn't get hurt last night?'

'Well, no – no, he's fine,' said Mum. 'It's just

Jack hasn't actually – *we* haven't actually tried dragging or pulling anything with him yet.'

Another man had come up while she was talking and, unbelievably, I realised it was Mr Hargreaves, our totally ancient teacher. He had his sleeves rolled up and was absolutely filthy and sweaty. I didn't know if he recognised me as I shrank back, but he simply said: 'Well, looks like now's the time to try,' in a very tired way, and then turned and went back to his sawing.

'We'll be back as fast as we can, with the horse,' said Dad firmly, and swung around in the water, sending a soaking wake over me and Mum as we floundered after him.

15

Horse Power

It seemed a much quicker walk back, but then I suppose it was, as we were half running and we weren't stopping to look at everything. I hardly had time to think, let alone worry. Dad swung off suddenly down the lane opposite the one leading to the Simpsons', and I hadn't the faintest where he was going, but me and Mum charged after him. There was a hedge, and a wide, low gate in front of a neat gravel drive, and behind that we saw a figure standing by a huge, felled tree trunk which lay in front of his garage door. He turned when he heard our feet, and I recognised him as the man I'd glimpsed cowering behind the wheel of the ambulance on the day the mob had attacked it.

Two more men appeared from the back of the house with ropes as we hurried up the drive. 'We've sawn through the thing, it's just shifting it now,' said the ambulance driver, running his hands through his hair. 'The stupid thing is, I keep feeling if only I had the ambulance, I could drag it with that! Then of course that's the point – to get the ambulance out! We'll need it for Mr Prince, if he's alive by the time we get to him.'

'We've found ropes,' said one of them, a short, sturdy man. 'We'll try our hardest, Joe.'

'Leave it if it doesn't move,' said Mum. 'We're coming back with the horse. It's not worth you injuring yourselves.'

'A horse!' said the other man, who was taller but less sturdy than the first. 'You have a horse? We'll get the thing done with that, all right. Did you hear that, Joe? I told you all that sawing was worth it.'

'Back as soon as we can,' said Dad, and we were off again. I would have enjoyed the feeling of having something everyone needed if only I was confident that Van would cope. If only I'd had the chance to try him out without blinkers, dragging about an old tyre, like the book suggested. Mum seemed to sense what I was thinking.

'Don't worry, Jack,' she panted, as we reached

Michael's gate. 'Like that old man said at the Princes', now's the time to try. It's not towing a cart. It's pulling a big tree. Even if Van doesn't like it much, he can't run off or anything – he pretty much *has* to drag it, if he's attached to it.'

Around the back of Michael's house, then I was through the field gate and calling Van, who was luckily only metres away. Meanwhile, Mum dragged the harness out of the outhouse and dropped it in a heap by the fence, picking out the bridle and passing it to me as Van approached.

'Drat, I forgot the headcollar,' I said. 'I just hope I can get this on.' First, I remembered to unbuckle the blinkers. I cast them on the ground. Van stood politely waiting. Whether this was because he sensed I was in deadly earnest, or whether there were still traces of sugar left on the bit, I have no idea, but he almost seem to lower his big bay head helpfully as I slipped the bridle on, and this time there was no battling with the bit – it just seemed to end up in his mouth, almost without my trying. I scooped up the metres of reins from the ground so Van didn't tread in them, and led him towards the fence and the rest of the harness. Michael and Em were there now, and I could hear Dad explaining what was going on.

They looked worried, but Michael called across to me: 'He'll be fine, Jack. We were going to say we'd help you try without the blinkers this afternoon in any case – I came and checked it would be all right with your dad this morning, after you went.'

'Oh,' I said, as I slipped the collar over Van's head. 'Thanks.' This morning seemed so long ago, now. But it felt good to know that whatever I'd thought about Simon's verdict, everyone else had faith in me and Van.

'And another thing,' said Em. 'I meant to point something out to you. Your mum and dad follow right up behind Van with the wheelbarrow, every day, when they're clearing the field of manure. I know it's not the same as him being attached to it, but he certainly sees it and it never frightens him.'

'That's true!' said Mum, and Dad nodded.

'I must admit, I never thought of him kicking out when we've got the barrow,' Dad said. 'I even bumped into him once. He didn't react at all.'

'Well,' I said, running the reins through the eyelets on the collar, and checking the last straps were all done up safely, 'as Mum said, this isn't even going to be a cart, just some heavy old timber. He'll have a job charging off, even if he wants to – and if he kicks out, he'll probably just hit the tree and no one else. It's now or never.'

Michael opened the gate and stood back.

'We'll come along and see how you get on. If he does kick it to pieces, we could do with the wood anyway, for the stove.'

'Ha, ha,' I said, leading Van past him. 'You haven't seen the size of it. There won't be pieces of wood if he kicks it; there'll be pieces of horse.'

'Go on, get on with the job and stop talking about it,' said Em. 'People are waiting for you.'

They haven't got a lot of choice, I thought, out in the lane with Dad walking along the other side of Van, particularly not poor Mr Prince.

Van pricked his ears and stared around him at the naked hedges, the clothing in the branches, the battered little bodies of birds. I went behind him, for the first time since his terrible display, and clicked my tongue and drove him properly. Dad stayed at the side of his head, one hand at the ring of the bit.

'Don't chivvy him too much, Jack,' he said. 'I know we're in a hurry, but you said he's frightened of what he can't see. Let him look a little if he wants. It was weird for us too, remember – we took a good look at everything. We don't want him to arrive feeling all worried.'

He was right, of course, so as Van walked along I talked away so he knew I was there and everything was fine, but when he slowed to stare at something, I let him take a good look before we walked on.

When we turned right to go to the ambulance man's house, he faltered a little in surprise as we'd never gone this way before, but he walked on nicely to the gate and I swear he looked rather pleased at the welcoming cries from the men.

They had padded the ropes with old bits of material and put them across their chests; they held out their hands to show us the marks there where they had pulled their hardest. But the tree had hardly budged a centimetre.

'Back him up to it and we'll tie the ropes on to the harness,' Dad said to me. 'And they'll all keep a hold of the tree as it moves so there's no way it can jump forward and hit his back legs or anything.'

I couldn't imagine, looking at the size of it, that it was about to jump forward or even move at all, however much Van tried to pull it, but I didn't say anything. I noticed he was staring at the tree and realised that he seemed to know when something wasn't in its right place – that's why he'd been worried about all the debris on the way here. I didn't know what the men would think, but I led him forward to look at the tree closely, and he snorted fearfully at first, but then reached forward with his nose and sniffed it, and immediately looked almost bored.

'Yes, it's just a tree,' I said. 'Like in the field. Only it's here on the ground, for some reason.' The ambulance man smiled.

'Not like the old tractors, are they?' he said. 'Got

feelings, a point of view. Well, does his lordship agree to give it a try?'

'He does indeed,' I said, and turned Van around to face the gate. The men passed their ropes to Dad and he threaded one through each keeper on either side of the harness, ending by knotting them to the rings on the collar. I stood to one side and slightly behind Van, out of the way of the tree trunk and clicked my tongue and chucked at the reins. Van took a few steps forward, felt the ropes tighten and stopped, confused.

Dad took hold of the bit ring and said, 'Come on, Van, come on,' and this reminded me to carry on with my clicking. Van tried to walk forwards again, felt the weight acting as a brake behind him, dithered slightly and lunged from one side to the other, then leaned into the collar and put his head down and took a step, then another, and I heard the timber scrape and roll. The ambulance man and the other men cheered, which seemed to have an effect on Van. I saw his back legs crouch down, like a runner in the starting blocks, then he pushed off the ground and lunged forwards again, and this time kept going, the huge trunk sliding along the ground easily, pushing a wave of gravel in front of it.

'Swing him right, on to the garden!' called the ambulance man, and my dad swapped sides and I dragged in the right rein, so that Van powered on to the turf, cutting out great clumps with his hooves, and the log swung across behind him to lie by the side of the drive. I realised I hadn't really believed we were going to move the thing, so hadn't thought where to drag it. If we had gone straight on, it would end up jammed across the gateway to the lane.

'Stop! That'll do!' called Dad, and I gathered up both reins and Van immediately stood still. The men ran forward to undo the ropes as we stood waiting. I was trying to look casual, like Dad, who seemed not at all surprised at our success, but inside my heart was bursting with pride. Van had pulled like he knew exactly what to do – and what strength! Of course I had seen Van's power in his wild displays, but I hadn't imagined what sort of weight he could move when that power was harnessed.

'We'll see you at the Princes',' my dad called back as we headed out of the gate. There was no time to be lost.

Was it my imagination, or did Van seem to walk with more confidence now, as I followed on behind the broad hindquarters and the swinging tail? Even though the pulling game had been new to him, he wasn't at all worried by it, it seemed. Nothing caused him to stop and stare on our way to the Princes': not the twisted metal and bits of machinery, the books and clothes and toys in the trees and hedgerows, not even the body of a dead dog in a ditch, which I hadn't noticed before.

So we arrived at our next job with Van striding in his new, assured way, and we caused quite a stir. A little way up the street from the back of the shop, parked just above the flood level, was a sparkling fuel-cell motorbike, in the bright colours of the emergency services, with PARAMEDIC written down both sides. I had hardly ever seen one before, and there was a crowd of kids around it, but they all looked up and rushed over to Van when we appeared.

'Wow!' said one of them to me. 'I wouldn't have recognised him. You've done some work! Wait till Dad sees him – I bet he won't believe what he traded for a pile of deer meat. I'm so sick of eating it, I swear I won't complain about pork, pork and nothing but pork ever again.'

And I suddenly realised it was Fred Simpson who was speaking. He didn't look like I remembered him. He had a cheeky, pleasant face and a snub nose and he was grinning at me in a way which reminded me of Jim.

'Oh – well, thanks,' I said. 'Just took a bit of brushing and some grass. We've come to try and shift this tree. We've done the one which was blocking the ambulance in. But this one's a lot bigger.'

'Come on,' said Dad. 'The paramedic's here, the ambulance will be here soon, and Mr Prince isn't going anywhere till we get this done. Hope Van's OK wading in this water.'

'I'm coming to watch,' said Fred firmly, 'though the paramedic told me to mind his bike for him. I'll get one of the others to do that.' And he sprinted off.

I clicked at Van and we walked on, around to the back of the shop. As we reached the edge of the shallow water, which Van could see was more than a puddle, he stopped, pricked his ears and tilted his head from side to side, inspecting. Dad went to his head and walked alongside and Van, reassured he wasn't about to plunge into a river, reluctantly sloshed forwards.

Through the open delivery gates in the wall we went, into what had once been the Princes' yard and was now a dirty lake. Again, I marvelled at how big the tree was. Its upended roots, still dangling boulder-sized lumps of orange earth, seemed taller than a house. The massive trunk, across the middle of the building, was part hidden inside the shop, but the bough which held the door closed was so thick that it seemed you'd need three men to span their arms around it, and it looked as long as the High Street. Men and women were dotted about like strange, dirtily dressed monkeys all over it; ropes came from different parts of it and went everywhere, even to the top of a telegraph pole.

'You know something?' I said to Dad. 'I just

realised I don't remember seeing this tree near the Princes' house.'

'It wasn't,' said my dad, 'or it would have been cut down, under the government's Storm Law rules. The tornado picked it up from right over there,' he pointed to the woods behind, 'and dropped it here. Sucked it right out of the ground.'

I looked at him. 'Some tornado,' I said. 'We were lucky, weren't we?'

Two figures came towards us. It was Mr Hargreaves, even more dirty and tired than before and, unbelievably, Mr Butt, the other teacher. His floppy hair was no longer excitable, but dripping and stuck to his head.

'Great. You're here,' he said, with a bit of his old spirit, but he wasn't quite clapping his hands and saying we were now cooking with gas. In fact, this was a whole new, serious Mr Butt. He reached out a hand towards my dad, then paused and looked at it and wiped it on his trousers before offering it again.

'You must be James Crosby. I understand you're a civil engineer,' he said, and my dad nodded. 'I'm

Tobias Butt, I teach at the school. I've done some calculations and we've attached rope and cable as best we can under the circumstances. If you'd like to come and take a look before we get started?'

Dad waved his hand. 'No, no, I trust you entirely. I already saw some of the ropes in place earlier and it looks sound enough.'

Mr Butt was gazing at Van.

'He's not exactly a Shire, is he? I had to work with what I knew . . . but he won't be taking the full weight, just getting the thing to start moving. We've sawn the smallest section we can get away with to get the door free. Everyone will be at the ends of the ropes, and they will pull and direct it, making sure it can't hit the horse, driver or anyone else. We've taken it over the telegraph pole and that will cope with some of the strain – I hope.' Suddenly, he spotted me.

'My goodness,' he said. 'If it isn't . . . Of course – Crosby. Jack would be your son,' he went on, looking at Dad. 'So this is what he's been up to instead of coming to school!'

Dad looked a bit awkward, but Mr Butt and Mr

Hargreaves smiled and waved their hands dismissively in the same way he had.

'Can't complain,' said Mr Hargreaves. 'He hasn't exactly been wasting his time, and he's here now. You ready, Jack?'

'Yes,' I said. I had no idea what was going to happen with all their plans and calculations, but I was happier now it sounded as if Van wasn't expected to move the mighty thing by himself.

At that moment, there was a slight commotion at the window by the back door. A group of people hurried over to someone calling from inside. One of them broke away and ran towards us. It was Fred.

'Hurry,' he gasped, splashing breathlessly. 'The paramedic says there isn't much time.'

'Watch out,' I said, then: 'Go on, Van. On you go.' Van didn't mind moving in the water now. I think he found anything better than standing still in it while people talked. We sloshed along until we came almost to the door, then I turned him hard right so that he ended up facing away from it.

As Dad pointed to the parts of the harness where

ropes could be fastened, I heard someone call out, and there were Harry Acre and Jim wading towards us, each dragging a piece of long chain which disappeared into the water behind them.

'No good tying rope on like that,' explained Harry, when he got alongside. 'The rope may break and, if not, this sort of weight will just tear the loops right off the harness.'

Of course it would – what were we thinking? If *I* felt stupid, my dad, the civil engineer, and Mr Butt, the maths teacher, looked especially shocked and embarrassed.

'It's all right, I got logging chains ready from my place. There's a swingletree on the back. We'll get him ready in a jiffy.'

I had no idea what he was talking about and I doubt if anyone else had, but I gathered up the reins and got out of the way, standing up by Van's head while they dragged the thing behind him and pushed the chains through the loops and clipped them securely to the collar. Another thing we hadn't practised at home. I patted Van and talked to him.

'It's a swingletree, horse,' I said. 'Swingletrees

are great. They are trees which grow swingles, your favourite type of sweet.'

Someone giggled next to me.

'You are bonkers, Jack Crosby. What if he decides to turn round and eat the swingles?'

It was Fred, with his face red from laughing.

'*You* are bonkers, Fred Simpson,' I answered, 'for believing the horse can understand me. What is it, anyway, this thing?'

'Dunno,' he said. 'Look, they're lifting the other end out of the water. Just a bar across and then bigger chains.'

Harry Acre and Jim Simpson bent in front of the massive branch, and the rust-red links of chain poured and dripped as they hauled them from the water and began to fasten them.

Then Harry stood back and put up his hand as if in a signal, and looked to me: 'Get behind him but to the side, not between the chains – drive him forward when I drop my hand. Got that?'

I nodded and sloshed round into position. Fred hovered next to Dad, who had taken Van's bit ring in his hand.

Then Harry looked up and around at all the dotted, perching figures surrounding us.

'Everyone ready? Got hold of your ropes?'

There were answering cries.

Harry dropped his hand.

'Go!'

I slapped the reins on Van's back and clicked as loud and as long as I could. Dad surged forward as Van lunged, so it looked like both of them were doing the pulling. The slack in the reins was taken up for a moment, but I only needed to move a step forwards. Van hadn't got anywhere.

'Again! Keep going!' shouted Harry from somewhere behind me.

'Go on, Van, go *on*,' I called, and I saw his ears go back and he crouched again, as I'd seen before, like a panther about to spring, and then made a tremendous lunge forwards.

I felt the reins almost snatched from my hands and, remembering that they led to the metal bit in his mouth, I ran forward, anxious not to hurt him. The water dragged at my legs and I almost fell over. At the same time, there was a huge splash behind me, and a wave surged and slapped me at the back of the legs. A great cry went up all around me and I saw Dad, at Van's head, stagger sideways and then he had to let go as Van charged onwards and past him.

I realised the cries were of 'Go, go!' and 'Pull now, pull!' so I didn't try to stop Van, but managed to get a better hold of the slipping, soaking reins and made every noise I could think of to keep him going – hissing, clicking and calling his name.

With every plunging step Van took, the slopping wave hit me from behind, as we towed the great piece of bough through the water. People were still shouting, but suddenly I heard a clear voice I knew through them all, and maybe I heard it because I didn't expect it to be there.

'OK, Jack! Stop! You can stop!'

It was Michael. I looked ahead, half blinded by my dripping hair, and saw him standing ahead of us in the gateway with his hands cupped around his mouth, shouting.

I shook the hair out of my eyes, tightened up my reins and yelled, 'Whoa, Van, whoa, now. Stand.' I didn't have to ask again. Van stopped. He turned his big bay head and stared at me – relieved, it seemed. His flanks heaved and steam rose up.

I wiped my face with my sleeve, which was filthy and soaking. People seemed to be hurrying everywhere – a woman was undoing the chains from Van's collar; more people, carrying a stretcher, passed behind me; the figures who'd been dotted about the fallen tree and the roof dropped their ropes and jumped down.

I turned and looked behind me. The great section of branch was lying half submerged, the door was open, and then, at last, the stretcher reappeared with someone lying on it, huddled beneath a red blanket. And there was Mrs Prince, wading behind it as fast as she could, her once-elegant outfit soaking and muddy and her hair loose and flying. As they went past, I saw Mr Prince. He looked ashy and asleep, but I felt sure he wasn't dead, as they hadn't covered up his face. Mrs Prince caught up as they came alongside me and Van, and grabbed at Mr Prince's hand from under the blanket.

'Raymond!' she pleaded, with tears streaking her face. 'Raymond! Speak to me!'

To my amazement, Mr Prince's eyelids fluttered and, for a moment, he gazed upwards. 'Ah,' I heard him say. 'You give in, then. Apology accepted. I'll speak to you now, Alicia.'

And they were whisked onwards and away amongst the stretcher bearers, to the ambulance now waiting on the road.

16

Ends and Beginnings

<u>April 27th continued</u>

We'd seen tornado damage before, of course, but not so much as this. I couldn't understand why there was a bit of a flood, at first, as there hadn't been *that* much rain, surely? Then Em pointed out that the hail had been so heavy and quick in falling it had blocked the drains, and this had been part of the reason the water hadn't got away.

The funny thing about the storm damage was, all the great posh houses didn't look quite so posh any more, and when we got home later, our old cottage didn't look quite so shabby.

We got down to the Princes' place at last – we must have arrived when Van was still dealing with the ambulance man's tree. When I stood there with Em and Jack's mum, watching as Jack guided and coaxed Van to pull that huge piece of timber, the waiting was all worthwhile. We'd watched the paramedic go in, and the tension was almost unbearable. Mr Prince was lying there, crushed, the life blood seeping out of him, but there was nothing anyone could do until the horse and his driver arrived. People busied themselves with ropes and cables, preparing for the moment it would be moved, making sure the great, shifting weight didn't swing or crash and hurt someone else. But we could do nothing but watch and wait.

We heard Van's hooves at last, and there they were – Jack's dad beside the frosted red coat of the horse and Jack walking along, driving him from behind. Jack was no bigger than when we'd first met, I'm sure, but the expression on his face, the way he held himself, he seemed to have grown. He looked more the man he would become and less the boy he'd been.

I was going to call him, as he hadn't seen us, standing up on the side of the road out of the water, but then I saw Fred Simpson run to him and the two of them were talking – in a friendly way, it seemed. I smiled at Jack's mum, standing alongside me, and she smiled back. This was what Jack needed –

friends who went to school. We didn't say anything, but stood and watched.

I had the strangest feeling when I saw that brave horse lunging and battling to move the great bough. My heart lifted in my chest and I fought with him – and when it moved at last, and Jack frowned and encouraged Van on, I felt none of the old feelings of powerlessness, of uselessness, of watching others doing what I couldn't. I felt as if I had played a part in everything building to this moment, and I was proud, terribly proud.

When I saw that Jack didn't hear people calling for him to stop now, the tree had moved far enough, I realised I couldn't bear Van to pull for a moment longer, so I called out – and at once Jack heard me and looked up through his soggy hair, and I smiled as the fierceness in his eyes evaporated into relief.

Me and Em and Jack's mum all hugged as if it was a sporting event and our champions had won. I don't know if they felt exactly the same as me at that moment, but I knew I'd just watched something important. Van had found his place, and so had Jack – and somehow, in helping out, I've found my place again, a part I can play, if only for a little while.

And for Jack, I know it is just the start.

Michael's writing stops there. I turn over the page, just in case, but there aren't any more entries – this time, I don't think he left blanks because things were boring, like when he was ill, but because we were too busy. Michael was right – it *was* the start, though I still have a long way to go and I don't know what's yet to come – but that isn't scary, it's exciting.

The day after the tornado, Fred was on my doorstep in the morning. 'I'm coming to see if you want to walk to school,' he said.

'Well . . . I don't know,' I said awkwardly.

'Oh, go on. It's been much better, lately. Mr Butt's maths lessons are brilliant fun now. We do maths hopscotch outside – you have to do a sum and jump to each answer – and we agreed on condition he does it as well, and it's hilarious, he just has no coordination. Then we do darts . . .'

'Darts?'

'Yes, he says the scoring system is great for

maths. We all promised to be sensible if we could use real darts, not the Velcro ones, because they were dud and just kept falling off. And it's gone fine, hardly anyone's been hurt, and then it was only Pottsy because he forgot the rule about walking across the shooting line, and he has such a wooden head it hardly made a mark anyway . . .'

'Wow,' I said.

'And then we finish up with mental maths bingo, and I've won twice already. And old Hargreaves seems better too – we're doing stories about our ancestors, it's brilliant. So you should come,' he finished up firmly.

I looked at his pleading expression. I realised he'd had to walk out of his way, in the opposite direction from school, to call on me.

'Well, all right. I'll give it a go. The teachers didn't seem so bad yesterday, really, when it was sort of real life. I'll just tell Mum and get my jacket.'

And so I went back to school, and Fred was right – the maths was fun, and seemed easy, and when it came to the reading and writing part, I did my best, and Mr Hargreaves said, 'Well, well, I'd hardly believe this was the same student's work, Mr Crosby. You must have been unsettled by the move when you first came here. You should have told me. Very well done, well done indeed.' And he gave me the highest mark I'd ever had.

A few days later, we borrowed the swingletree again, and Michael helped me harness Van to the boat trailer, and we took *Aunt May* down to Harry Acre's cartwright's shop and we left her there, to be turned into the most beautiful tradesman's cart you ever saw, all polished and curved, with the old name made part of the writing on the side, so it now reads: *Aunt May's Finest – Fruit and Veg, Fresh to Your Door.*

All that was Michael's idea, too. He'd said now that Van could pull things safely, shouldn't we get a cart? Mum had said that there was no money to buy one, but though it would hurt, after the boat had saved our lives, she and Dad thought maybe they should sell *Aunt May* as she was no longer needed, and use the money to buy a cart. But it would be tricky to transport her for any distance to sell, and it would cost so much they might not get much money back at the end of it. So Michael had said, 'Why not just recycle her? Harry could do it quite cheaply,' so that's what we did. We were all happier that we still had *Aunt May* and she was still helping our family.

We were soon growing enough vegetables to be able to sell some, and Michael helped pack up the boxes, and the colours of it all looked beautiful, as if the cart was decorated; the scarlet flash of tomatoes, red peppers and chillies, warm to the touch, against glistening wet emerald salad leaves; chestnut and white strings of onions and garlic; thin fingers of green and yellow beans laced over fat globe artichokes, and squashes and melons of every colour under the sun. And when you added the boxes of strawberries, the delicious waft of burnt-sugar candyfloss they gave off would bring wasps and children swarming. Then we'd haul ourselves up, me in the driver's seat and Michael behind, and we drove along the lanes, calling door-to-door and meeting everyone. They all seemed to know Michael, and he was a great favourite with the old ladies for some reason.

Sometimes we'd pass Simon and Spud, and Simon, who had been quite embarrassed that his advice about the blinkers had proved to be wrong, had got over it, and we called out friendly insults to each other about who had the best horse: 'When's it going in the freezer then?' (from Simon) and: 'A spud should be in the ground or on a plate,' (from me), but I admit I found that one hard to come up with because, of course, I'd always be fond of Spud because it was meeting him which led me to wanting to save Van.

We made a great team, me and Michael, and I don't know why I thought it would go on for ever. If I'd stopped and thought, I'd have realised it wasn't possible, of course. Things always change.

They changed one evening when Em and Michael had sat down and chatted after their meal, and Em went around locking up and switching things off before bed, and when she came back, Michael was asleep already in his chair. Except he wasn't asleep.

The first I heard about it was a murmur at the

front door – I don't even remember hearing anyone knock – and then I thought I heard a sob. I came downstairs and found the front door open. Dad was standing in the hall, not doing or saying anything, with a weird, blank look on his face.

'What's the matter?' I said. 'Who was that? Where's Mum?'

Dad told me Mum had gone with Em, it was about Michael, and we waited around and the news came back with Mum much, much later.

While Mum stroked my hair as I cried, she tried to say all the right things to make me feel better, like the fact that Michael was, after all, eighty years of age, and it was amazing how he'd recovered from the flu which had killed so many, and had all that time, time he'd enjoyed with me and Van, which Em really wanted me to remember.

You might think it's odd that I had to be reminded that Michael was an old man, but he'd changed a lot from when I'd first met him, pale and tired in his wheelchair, and I had sort of forgotten. When you got to know him, it wasn't something you noticed, it just wasn't important.

It was good, in a way, that I cried and cried when I heard, because it meant I got it out of my system and did manage to hold on to some dignity at his funeral.

It was after that that Em came up to us and told me Michael wanted me to have his last diary, and to remember that it had been his dearest wish that we would always have the land from their cottage to use for Van, and so she'd promised him and made sure it was included in her will – we weren't to worry. And I'd just looked at her blankly, because I'd lost Michael, and I couldn't care about a diary or think about the land and the future.

But days later, she'd brought the diary, and I'd been desperate for it. It was, I'd realised, something of Michael, his voice, his thoughts, that I could have and share and hold on to for ever. Now I've read it, I realise how much more it has told me – about Michael, about myself, about everyone.

I hope you enjoyed it too.